'This deeply humane novel, about an intricate relationship between born-heres and from-aways in a small Maine town, left me breathless, wordless, and grateful to be part of the human family. The story is riveting, the prose hypnotic. Lewis treats his flawed, beautiful characters with both a ruthless honesty and a rare generosity. I needed fifteen minutes to recover myself after I turned the final page. I'm sorry this blurb is inadequate. Let me just say: Unforgettable. I feel changed.'

Monica Wood, author of *The One-in-a-Million Boy*, *When We Were the Kennedys*, and *Ernie's Ark*

'Lewis takes us deep into the strange and conflicted heart of the imagined Maine community of Sneed's Harbor. But this is more than a quaint story of locals and city folks; in Lewis's world, all the most modern moral vectors – of race, class, gender, and technology – are at play, offering us a new way of understanding how even our most idyllic dreams of reinvention and redemption are never exempt from the very real and difficult gravity of the world. Land of Cockaigne is a beautifully written and highly inventive testament to grief, place, longing, and love.'

Jaed Coffin, author of *A Chant to Soothe Wild Elephants* and *Roughhouse Friday*

T0018493

Jeffrey Lewis has won a string of awards for his novels including the Independent Publishers Gold Medal for Literary Fiction, the Independent Publishers Gold Medal for General Fiction, and the ForeWord Book of the Year Silver Medal for Fiction. His most recent book, *Bealport: A Novel of a Town*, was a 2019 Maine Literary Awards finalist. He has also received two Emmy Awards and been nominated twelve times for his work as a television writer and producer, most notably for *Hill Street Blues*.

LAND OF COCKAIGNE

First published in 2021 by
HAUS PUBLISHING LTD.
4 Cinnamon Row, London SW11 3TW

This paperback edition published in 2023

ISBN 978-1-913368-70-8
eISBN: 978-1-913368-17-3

Cover image by Gayle Lewis

Typeset in Garamond by MacGuru Ltd

Printed in the United Kingdom by CMP

Distributed in North America by The University of Chicago Press

A CIP catalogue for this book is available from the British Library

www.hauspublishing.com

LAND OF COCKAIGNE

A Novel

JEFFREY LEWIS

The Arrival

In September the bay freshens and the tourists go back to the cities and there are days when the eagles come back and the air smells of burnt things and things beginning to die. These are days when heaven can wait and there are men in the woods practicing their guns and on such a day, as if the shotgun blasts reverberating from Half Bush Island to Caitlin's Point were fireworks for the dispossessed, the lonely, and those who have only just come home, Walter Rath and Catherine Gray sailed their white yawl by the head and through the channel and into Sneeds Harbor. She would stay and have her child there and they would stay longer and their child would go to school there and after awhile they sailed down the coast on the yawl less. They weren't the sort of people ever to say they were happy, for whispers of the gods and retribution, but others said it for them and of them, as if the little village past the channel had landed a special prize. She went by Charley, people had always called her Charley.

The computers and all of it had reached the village and it wasn't long before who Walter Rath was was known and nods went his way and Charley's. She was pregnant then and that was part of it too, she was even prettier when she was pregnant which was saying something it was said, though there was no one at the post office or in the store then who'd seen her when she wasn't. She was fit and wore all the gifts and her honey hair had the girls of Sneeds talking of salons they would never see. Even her posture, the way she held tall, carrying that child, as if it was

1

weight she'd been born for. And in the store they talked of Walter Rath's money.

No one knew and it was all a guess. Once you talked in millions or billions it was all the same anyway, words lost their gravity and floated by. Not a little envy was stirred, or it could have been plain dirt fear, that he would take his marbles back west, or buy up the town, or his cronies would come in and the prices of everything would go up. But the cronies never arrived and then there came the thought that Walter Rath didn't have them, that he was some kind of lone gunner from a world where there were things stronger and bigger than guns. The truth in any of it was that Walter Rath had gone out there when the Valley was young and when there were boys still in their garages and there'd been no one in a suit and a tie who picked the winners better than he did. He'd picked Jobs and more than a couple of others, and then he was on television, the honored guest, the sage of San Jose, and punters in Duluth or Tallahassee would tune in to listen to who he was touting next. Then he was done with all of it, so that he was gone almost before the whole thing was up and running crazy big and spoken of with reverence. He was an early one. He'd left money on the table. And he'd met Charley by then, who'd been around the Valley herself and with some of the boys too, in her own fashion, the It girl of the Valley for awhile, and they'd both had enough. He bought the Concordia in Monterey Bay where it was rare and they sailed until they couldn't or wouldn't anymore. When they saw Sneeds Harbor on the chart, Charley said, "What a funny name."

They put the boy in the school that had seven in his class and five of them were girls. The school was on the common with the Civil War monument and those of the elms that had survived the elm plague and it was white clapboards like the house they bought two blocks away. Soon after the house, they bought the

2

old summer camp on the bay that was two hundred twenty acres and she went out there to ride and sculpt. The camp was at the edge of the town. It had broken buildings from when it was the summer camp and ghost stories faint in the walls. It was the boy's favorite place. He would get lost in the spruce woods and Charley would yell before it was dark and each time, every time, he followed his mother's voice out.

The way it started with Walter Rath in the town was that he would go in the store and sit at the table by the back by the sodas with his *Times*. There were five stools at the counter where the men of Sneeds sat and occasionally Doris Bunting too. They could swivel around and get a casual look at him and he could see them but he would never take their stools, it being a question equally of respect and calculation. And they never read the *Times,* the joke about the tourists who came all the way past Bar Harbor in the summer being that if they had to have their *Times* they could just go back to New Yawk where they came from. But Rath hadn't come in summer. Nor had he been in New York, not lately anyway, except to sail the white yawl up the East River and under the bridges and out into the Sound, the city as a sweet little detour. And his *Times* came by mail, a day late.

Maggie Lassiter who had the store after Ed Lassiter keeled over, so it was said from too many of her French fries, made nodding acquaintance of Rath when he dropped a dollar in the jar each time he paid. Neither too little nor too much, which was Walter Rath's way. Bob Pearce had a conversation with Rath about PVC versus copper that impressed Bob for the man's practicality, as opposed, say, to the summer people over in Hancock or Winter Harbor who Bob had heard about from the plumbers over there and who put copper in no matter what, because copper was copper and who cared what it cost. Cal Bowden at the boatyard dreamed fever dreams of getting his hands on the Concordia and when Rath sailed it over to Northeast for winter storage you could say Cal was not amused, but then there was always something to unamuse Cal Bowden and one day Rath stopped in to buy a case of Yamalube and was even-natured and spent the time of day and Cal came back to his fevered dreams of the white yawl, if now situated somewhere over the rainbow. Others had pleasant, measured experiences as well, at the post office, in the Red & White, and it was by such undramatic encounters, where nothing exceptional could be pointed to or made gossip, that Walter Rath seeped into the capillaries of Sneeds Harbor, such that by Christmas he and Charley were lighting candles on Church Street bundled against the wind chill with all the rest. Soon after, there were townspeople unafraid, if they saw him in the store and their Mac had frozen or died or the screen was the blue of the ocean, to ask him for his help. These were not things Walter Rath knew about but he never failed to be regretful, saying "sorry" in his low, sad voice.

And so Walter and Charley were special in Sneeds Harbor and the more so for not seeming it. They were the Walter and Charley who baked breads for the church fairs and drove the seniors to the polls and manned booths on the Fourth of July and could be counted on to give for the ambulance and the library and the preschool enrichment and whatever else, but not so much that they would take captive these things that were properly of the town in whole. In their fifth year in Sneeds Harbor, about the time the boy entered the school, Walter was elected to the Board of Selectmen. Still, no one ever called him "Walt."

A Son's Siddhartha Moment

The Cormers lived in a single wide four miles out of Sneeds down the trailer park road. As trailers went it wasn't a bad one, a Fleetwood Festival with floors that flexed only with the rains and wall paneling stained over by Donnie himself so that it could almost be mistaken for wood. They were a one-kid family like the Raths and out of a stroke of fortune Kevin Cormer who was the caretaker's son was the other boy in the first-grade class of Stephen Rath so that they were best friends whether they wanted to be or not. They fended off the posse of girls and went their way, here and there, after school and sometimes weekends too, on bikes and foot and splashing around in the shallows where the Raths' camp edged the bay, but Stephen had never once been to visit at the Fleetwood Festival down the trailer park road. Donnie Cormer had become the Raths' caretaker their first year in Sneeds Harbor and he took care, as well, of a few of the summer people's houses over in Hancock, there being no summer colony in Sneeds to speak of; and he did a little mussel harvesting in the winter, being part of the local fraternity that, as it was said, did three jobs to make one living.

Kevin could show things to Stephen, being more advanced in country ways. He was a lanky, skinny boy with crooked teeth still coming in and he had a knife and Stephen didn't and there were other areas in his favor so that Stephen looked more up to him than the other way around. Stephen was darker and more careful and sometimes he watched where he stepped. He was more like his father and Kevin was more like his, as if nature was holding no secrets this time around. With his knife Kevin carved his initials and carved small boats to float here and there and he would let Stephen carve his initials too, on trees and benches and whatever presented itself, and they had the time together where it could seem to a boy there was nothing more to want in life, such that if it hadn't been for Freddie Coombs, Stephen might never have noticed that he'd not been down Kevin's road ever once. Freddie was in the second grade. The second grade also suffered a drought of boys, Freddie being the only one since the Whittles took Andrew Whittle away to Pennsylvania, and so Kevin and Stephen took pity on Freddie and played with him from time to time.

On a Saturday they were hypnotizing frogs and Freddie was tiring of it. He thought hypnotizing frogs was a first-grade thing to do, and he threw his frog back in the ditch. "Let's go to Kevin's house," he said.

"It's too far," Kevin said, holding tight to his frog in the fingers of one hand while the fingers of his other turned twitchy spirals, so that the frog stayed hypnotized.

"It's a trailer, you can move it," Freddie said. He was appealing to Stephen now.

"Does your house move?" Stephen said.

"It doesn't move," Kevin said.

"It could, it could, it's a trailer," Freddie insisted. "You could drive it somewhere."

"You couldn't," Kevin said.

"Can we go there?" Stephen asked, having never seen a house that moved.

The remaining frogs went back in the ditch and they rode their bikes on the Clarkswood Road and down the trailer park road, which was dirt and bounced their bikes, and got to the Cormers'

Fleetwood Festival which was on cinderblock and didn't look to Stephen like it could move. Like, would it fly, would it have secret wheels that came out?

"It doesn't move," Kevin said again. He was ready to leave and put his leg over his bike.

"Then it used to. You changed it," Freddie insisted.

Then Kevin said he didn't change it then Freddie said he changed it then Kevin said Freddie was a peeshit and Stephen hadn't heard the word before and wondered exactly what it meant, how it all went together. The trailer was painted white and had a TV antenna so that it looked to Stephen like a cake with an insect on top. Kevin's mother came out and called his name.

"We're going," Kevin said.

She said his lunch was ready and to bring his friends in.

"They're not hungry," Kevin said and pressed on the pedal of his bike so that he looked eager to race away, but the other boys' looks told otherwise and Kevin grimaced and so they all went in.

Stephen hadn't been in so small a house before and he liked it because it felt like a game, like you could go blindfolded in it or cook things yourself. There was a table and there was a window and these were small too. It was the right size for everything, Stephen thought. Caryn Cormer was pleased as she had only the one boy and now the boys were filling up her house. She made up two more sandwiches and was putting them on real plates, keeping up a patter now, mayo or mustard, sweet pickle or sour, and here's some chips and here's some milk. When she made lunch it was most often on paper plates, so there would be less washing to do, but these were guests, even though they were young. She knew who Stephen's parents were but that only went to show, and show what exactly?

Donnie came in in his boots and Caryn told him to take them off and Stephen said, "Hello, Mr. Cormer," and Donnie nodded in surprise and went to the end of the trailer where there was a door and went in and shut the door, and you could have heard when he took his boots off, when they hit the floor, so it must have been that he didn't. Stephen had been taught to call him "Mr. Cormer" because Donnie called his father "Mr. Rath" and it was the polite thing to say.

Caryn put the lunch in front of the boys, who were quiet now. Kevin and Stephen ate quickly but Fred picked at his food.

"It's the government cheese," Freddie said.

"It's not. It's American cheese," Kevin said.

"It's the government cheese," repeated Freddie, who lived in a real house with a front yard and back.

"It's American cheese!" Kevin raised his voice. "Isn't it, Mom? It's American cheese, right?"

Caryn said you could call it either one, because she didn't like her boy to be embarrassed nor did she like to lie.

"I told you! Liar!" Freddie said.

"I'm not! It's American!" Kevin shouted.

Stephen had never heard of the government cheese and didn't know it was the cheese you got from the government if you were poor. And it's possible, as well, that none of the boys knew what a government was. But Stephen heard the whine that streaked Kevin's shout. "It tastes like American," he said.

"See? *See?*" Kevin screamed at Freddie.

"Government cheese! Government cheese! Peeshit government cheese!" Fred sang in singsong.

Finally, when the boy's mockery wore down, Caryn asked Stephen if he liked it and was it okay, as if to appeal to the one neutral party, as if a King Solomon or one of those had descended on the trailer park, though he had eaten only half his sandwich.

"It's good," Stephen said, and for some reason he thought of Kevin's knife then.

"She bought it at a store!" Now Kevin's voice was hoarse and these sounded like all the words he could get out. He got up and ran down the trailer until he was through the door where his father had gone. The yellow cheese was in fact surplus cheese that came in a brick free from the state pantry in Bangor twice monthly.

"It tastes like American," Stephen said again.

He wished that Kevin would come back out through the door. The trailer seemed even smaller to him now, as if the walls had moved in like the walls in a scary movie he'd seen, yet it also felt empty, as his stomach felt empty, though he had eaten half the sandwich. He wished his friend not to be whatever way he was being, which was a way Stephen had not seen before, just as he had not felt empty in just this way before. He finished his sandwich and gobbled his chips and it didn't help.

Two Hours in the Bronx

At 8:39 p.m. he was making his spaghetti sauce which was something where he intended to show her the range of what he could do but there wasn't enough garlic and the bodega closed at eight, so he said he would go to the market that was open later. She said don't bother because he'd have to get in the car and why lose the parking space when they could have the whatever-the-pasta-was tomorrow but he said he wanted to do it tonight and all that was missing was a head of garlic.

At 8:43 he hadn't left and saw her in her bra and felt frisky and grabbed her arm as she passed by.

At 8:57 he lay in her arms and thought various thoughts about her that even he thought were too young, like was she the one, or something like the one, the closest thing yet to the one, the one being the part that was too young unless it was too old at the same time.

At 9:03 he lay in her arms and thought various thoughts about the kid in court that day whose smile was the crookedest thing about him but he'd had two chances in the program already and this time it was a grand larceny auto of a luxey one in Riverdale and the judge known to the program reps as Hang 'Em High Si Bernstein had said to the kid as he handed him four months at Rikers, "DeAndre, I'm getting tired of seeing you around here," which was fair enough since it was the kid's third time but what Stephen hadn't liked was the way the judge said "DeAndre" with too much space between each syllable so that it sounded like he was calling in a cat.

At 9:05 he lay in her arms and tried to make a list of all the judges they'd thought of stupid nicknames for, there was Hang 'Em High Si Bernstein, there was Give 'Em Hell Del Shaughnessy, there was Turn 'Em Loose Bruce Johnston and Make 'Em Pay Jay Levenson and Send 'Em Upstate Nate Gordy too, and was that all of them or were there more still to be named, he and Sharon sitting there between smiles trying to make the best of long days in court and more kids in trouble than getting out of it.

At 9:12 he lay in her arms and thought of DeAndre again, and if he'd had a name like Jim would he have got two months instead of four, or maybe even the program again, become a P for Participant again, because if you were a kid named Jim wouldn't you sound to a judge like you wanted to turn it around?

At 9:22 he lay in her arms and she stirred and her arm fell down his chest a little and tweaked him just because she felt like it and he felt frisky again.

At 9:33 they were again in an act of love, that was slow this time around so that every second lasted longer than it should and every touch carried with it the idea of a touch.

At 9:47 he lay in her arms and dreamed of a dry cleaners where he took his pants and when he went in it was the size of Yankee Stadium except all the players' uniforms were clean, even the ones who had slid home safe.

At 10:07 he lay in her arms and she nudged him a little and said the Fine Fare was going to close at eleven so he'd better get going if he was going.

At 10:09 he said fuck it, he'd make the sauce tomorrow, which was what she hoped he'd say and tugged him down.

At 10:11 he kissed her neck down low and got up and pulled on his pants because he was twenty-four years old and hungry and she said as long as he was going they needed paper towels and creamer for the coffee.

At 10:17 p.m. on the ninth of October, 2016 he grabbed the car keys and his phone and said he'd be home in an hour and double-locked the door when he left.

Aftermath

It was past the bad old days and crime was down enough that when a white kid of promise was gunned down in the Bronx it made all the papers, even the *Times*, and it led on the local news, so that when they arrived there was that too to contend with. At the hotel he was afraid to open the *Times* and he put it in the trash. They took a cab uptown to a street with a high number where it intersected an avenue they'd never heard of and sat at the curb that was as dirty as any other curb in the city but they sat there with their knees up and blank stares. What was there to look at, really? Pizza places, a check cash. Even the police tape was gone. Later they picked up the ashes and couldn't bear to pick out an urn.

On the news programs, too, was the irony of it all, that the victim of the carjack gone tragically wrong was in the Bronx to keep kids out of jail. If he hated anything then, Walter hated those ironies. What liberties these people took, what cheap pathetic lies to keep the ads coming. The carjacker was dead, killed by the cops in a chase that wound up the wrong way on the Cross Bronx cut-through. That, too, was a big story, a traffic story as well as a crime one. They could have left the city then, they could have had Stephen's things packed up and sent, but Charley wanted to see the girl.

So in the evening they went to the place that for three and a half months Sharon and Stephen had shared. It was on a block a few blocks from the Concourse that had once been notable for the number of Holocaust survivors who settled there. It was her apartment and he'd moved in, so that nearly everything in it was hers. He was twenty-four and traveling light. He met her because she hired him. She was older by seven years, which was the biggest surprise when they met her, as Stephen had told them that she was Black, but they could see at once she was older, on her face and in the way she moved, there was a slowed-down glide to her movements as if to suggest she'd lived longer with pain and now managed the world with greater care. She was tall, as tall as Stephen. She invited them in. The apartment was nondescript, a few prints on the walls, a few items that looked like Ikea. She'd put all Stephen's things in two boxes, the clothing in one, the other things in the other. The clothing was all folded, even the underwear lined up neatly in the box, as if it had just come from the Fluff 'n' Fold.

Neither of them liked that she was so prepared to be rid of Stephen's traces but then she said she didn't know what else to do so instead of screaming and waking the neighbors she'd gathered his things up from here and there, made a little inventory, and they liked the way she said that part, as she seemed as without defenses as themselves. She said she'd never imagined all his things could go in those two boxes, it was almost like he'd never really moved in, like it almost put the lie to something, but still she didn't think it was a lie. She offered them coffee which they declined. They looked around a little, though not so much it would seem they were prying into her life. The window looked out on other brick apartments, the whole block was brick apartments. She told them how he'd gone out for a head of garlic. Charley said, to Walter, "Would you mind if Sharon and I had a moment?" and he was happy she asked because it was a sign she was returning to life, a trite enough thought but when he tried to think it through better he failed because he wasn't that close to returning

16

to life himself. The women went in the bedroom. Walter peeked in the boxes. A couple of hoodies, a sweater with a zipper, the folded underwear and socks and jeans and a jacket and tie for the courthouse so that the Bronx Cares Diversionary Action Program would seem respectable. In the other box, his phone, his wallet, an envelope weighted with change, a few books, a scissors, a nail clipper, an eraser, several pencils bundled by a rubber band. When the women came out it was plain they'd shed tears, then there were good-byes and phone numbers and thanks and sorrys and she called them an Uber. They took the boxes and left and never said to each other whether they liked her or not. Nor did Sharon ask herself whether she liked them. There would have been no point to it.

Back in Sneeds the Raths did the things that were done by people in their situation, including not knowing what to call their situation so that they wouldn't be hurt further either by too much honesty or too many lies, the middle way of grief. They scattered his ashes in the bay by the camp and put a stone there and went to grief counseling in Bangor twice a week and held each other as often as they could and went through periods when they couldn't. They put on the best face with their neighbors and asked patience of them and Charley had coffees with her friend Rose Britton and Walter made all the selectmen's meetings. They answered whatever questions they had answers to, which weren't that many. In the spring they put the yawl in the water but didn't sail it. Likewise in the spring, past Memorial Day when the smatter of summer people filtered back, they arranged for a memorial at the Congo church so that the whole village turned out. It rained that day and Sally McMartin the minister gave a eulogy that was long on homily and analogy and sheer unlikelihood which Walter panned in his mind but said nothing about because the town in its democratic weight seemed to like it. Afterwards there was a rainbow which Charley said was a sign and Walter said he wasn't so sure.

Meanwhile in the store the village had expressed its concerns. There was the time Maggie Lassiter said she felt the whole thing had wounded her more deeply than him because you could see it in her eyes, she almost didn't blink anymore. Doris Bunting agreed about the wound but not because of her eyes or her blinking but because Charley was a mother after all, which the realtor who sold the Raths their camp, Paul Schissel, took issue with because just because fathers were silent didn't mean they suffered less and in some demonstrable cases, as for instance Job in the Bible, they clearly suffered more. You don't know how much Job's wife suffered, Maggie Lassiter said. On another occasion Donnie Cormer, as their caretaker of twenty-five years, spoke with authority and pronounced that it was all a question of time and you couldn't rush time. Then on another occasion Cal Bowden from the boatyard reported that they'd had the brightwork touched up on the boat, which to him indicated they were going to use it, if not the summer, he would guess, then the fall. Herbert Fallows, the retiree from the insurance agency who tended to dispute whatever Cal said, disputed him then because if you didn't keep the brightwork up you could lose the value of your boat, so it was more an automatic thing. That would be true for normal people, Cal replied, but you had to take in account that the Raths were rich as kings. Then Kevin Cormer, who had his own business now, trimming trees and the like, and who lived two towns east but still came into Sneeds for his coffee, reminded all who were sitting around that it was his friend Stephen and not the parents who died, and what was *that* like, to die? This had the effect of quieting everyone down. On still another occasion Iris Kearns opined that no marriage survives the death of a child. When she felt the room go cold, Iris then added that it was something she'd heard and that's what they say anyway, so she wasn't vouching for it herself, though it made a certain sense.

The Raths knew that they were talked about but they chose to take it more as love than gossip, or even as a small private joke, maybe their only little joke of those months, the silence that came over the store, not always but on several occasions, when one or the other of them walked in. After the memorial they tried and failed to make love, a stumbling, fumbling try after many months when they hadn't, then tried again and it was better, then she made omelets and they watched the news. As they watched, he had an arm lightly across her shoulder, which he often did when they watched the news these days, as if who could say what might come next that would need a measure of comfort. Then she felt there would not be a better time to tell him the idea she'd stored and nurtured, which had begun in the little conversation she'd had with Sharon Mason in the apartment in the Bronx. So she told him what Stephen had discussed with Sharon and Sharon had confided to Charley, his idea that kids from his program in the Bronx would come up to Sneeds Harbor and stay out at the camp for two weeks and all their needs would be attended to and they would be expected to do no more than not get in any really egregious trouble and they'd have lobster for dinner every night and be treated in general like little princes. And now Charley wanted to do this, she'd been thinking about it for months and been not sure and held off, all the time thinking, but it was Stephen's idea and it was a way now to honor him which would be more than a rock by the shore.

She got all of that out in gulps and bursts. It had been stored up and she so much wanted Walter to come along. First he was silent and she fretted and said then she'd do it herself if he wasn't interested. This was the kind of thing she said sometimes and she knew it would drive him crazy, it was so wrong and premature, jumping the gun out of what must have looked like fear, though she was never afraid of him, really, it was more that she didn't want to hate him for saying no.

When she thought of jumping the gun, she thought of the gun that killed their son. He removed his arm that had stayed around her until then. She was a little breathless as well. He chose not to look at her, but rather to look down at his hands, when he said, "The Land of Cockaigne."

The Land of Cockaigne

It was the old medieval peasants' dream, of chops for breakfast every morning and the skies raining sweet wine and the fish not needing to be caught because they jumped out of the water and landed in the net. Houses were made of sugar and the streets were cobbled with nuggets of gold and you could shit where you liked and nuns spread their legs for passing strangers. No work, no worry, no death. In Rath's rooms at Yale there'd been a print of Brueghel's painting of this land. A roommate had found it on the street and put it over the fireplace, where it either blessed with permission or warned of what the world might become.

Was the Land of Cockaigne really what Stephen had in mind? Of course not, Rath thought. But he couldn't think of another way to answer her. His words felt all boxed in and all he wanted was to keep her going.

The Talk of the Town

Maggie Lassiter would tell anyone who asked what she thought. Anyone, that is, with the obvious exceptions of Walter and Charley. When the rumor reached the store, by way of Donnie Cormer, that the Raths were going to pay to bring up young delinquents from New York City for what amounted when all was said and done to summer camp, Maggie felt at once that this had to be a situation where, despite their best intentions, and nobody was going to deny their best intentions, but still, the Raths were trying to work out their grief at the expense of good sense and the village. It would be one thing if they wanted to pay to have these people go to a summer camp close to New York City, but why bring them all the way up to Sneeds Harbor? She tried to remember so she could quote it from Mrs. Rundell's old history class about bringing coals to Newcastle, but once she was able to halfway state it, Doris Bunting pointed out that it did not apply and in fact meant almost the complete opposite of what Maggie was thinking.

Otherwise Doris found herself in some agreement with Maggie, in that these people would probably feel less alienated and possibly even homesick so far from home. Just imagine, for example, if you took Cal Bowden or Rine Worsley, some of those who'd never been farther than Bangor in their life, and suddenly sent them to summer camp in New York City, when they were younger of course, but how would they react?

Herbert Fallows went further than either of the women and

suggested there might even be some animosity being expressed here, though he wouldn't want to say by whom and up till now he'd been a big fan of the Raths. Along the same lines, one of the lobstermen, Tim Frobisher, wanted to know what exactly they were trying to prove.

Nothing, they're not trying to prove anything, Frances McVay replied, they're only trying to honor something Stephen wanted, that's how she read the situation. And by invoking the boy's name, a boy who went to the school and grew up in Sneeds with hardly an unkind word ever said about him, she hoped she would turn the tide of apprehension that seemed to be developing in the void created by the lack of real facts.

There were others of the "pro" persuasion in the store, for example Kerry Micheau, who cut hair on the Clarkswood Road and who pointed out that from what she heard it would only be two weeks and you can live with anything for two weeks, and Pat Morris, the town's all-purpose massage therapist, yoga instructor, and part-time Red & White sales associate, who simply felt that, in general, everyone should stop being so nitpicky and at least wait to see what developed.

Wait to see what develops, Bob Pearce said, and by then it could be too late. At minimum, he suggested, they should be finding the proper authorities in New York to inquire if they were going to be sending up any murderers. In fact, he'd do it himself, he'd figure out who to call, which would probably take all week which he didn't really have to spare in as much as the Canovers' septic required an immediate one hundred percent replacement, but he intended to do it regardless. Murderers, everyone agreed, would be going too far.

If Gallup had bothered to poll the town, they would probably have found it fairly evenly divided, like someone who parts his hair down the middle in an antique style. Harry Casey, who was considered by some the village radical or possibly libertarian and who had once run, decades previously and unsuccessfully, for the State Assembly as a peace candidate, pointed out that not only did the camp belong to the Raths and they should be able to do what they wanted on it, but if you remembered your Sneeds Harbor history you would see the beautiful irony that in the year 1895 or thereabouts there had been a hotel resort situated in what were now the backwoods of the Raths' camp, and that hotel had a housekeeping staff of Black people, which you could see pictures of at the Historical Society, showing ten of them in their uniforms. It was thought to be the only time so large a contingent of Black people had lived in Sneeds. Emily Thomas said she'd seen those photographs and they were quite touching and the Raths were wonderful people to be doing this and Sneeds ought to be doing its part to help out with a national problem. This quieted the store discussion for a few minutes. No one felt up to arguing with Em, though privately there were those who felt she had gone a bit mad since Graham passed and left her a million and a half dollars of untaxed lobster profits.

The Hypocrite

Walter had said to her "the Land of Cockaigne" which she found insufferable and just like Walter to tell her something he would then have to explain, but when he explained, it was again like Walter, she felt, to have a thought she would never have had in a hundred years and probably no one else would have had it either but still it didn't quite go away. She was wary of Walter's mind, that reminded her in her sootier moods of Clem, a smart and faithful and unusually helpful dog they'd had once, who every once in a while and for no apparent reason took a bite out of something or someone, the furniture or Aunt Geraldine. But he hadn't said no. So she set to work as if a ghost were chasing her and catching up and the safety of the car or the root cellar was still far off. She got bids on renovating the broken-down cabins of the camp, engaged a Bar Harbor lawyer to ascertain that no laws would be broken if they went ahead, and interviewed potential nurses and drivers and cooks. She spoke often with Sharon Mason, and with persons Sharon connected her to, to see how kids should be recruited, chosen, persuaded, and what they would need. When an issue arose with the court system, as to whether these juveniles diverted to the program could be permitted to leave the city and miss classes and appointments, she leaned on the Legal Aid Society to seek a waiver on the grounds that what was proposed would be not only a wholesome supplement to Bronx Cares but cost-free to the state. She also hired Sharon, with whatever title Sharon wanted, in the event this daydream actually got off the ground. It was easy, really, to do these things when you had money to spend.

In the meantime, Walter's mind squirmed. "Retreated to his study" might have been a more tactful or anyway rhetorical way to say it. He had often "retreated to his study." In the Valley he'd done it when they made "like" a noun, or anyway that was the tale that went around, a tale that wasn't quite right because "like" had always been a noun, maybe not as often as it had been a verb but often enough, so that perhaps what he had really objected to was "friend" becoming a verb, but anyway people got the point. The other formulation had been that he didn't like "like" being reduced to a digital button. Reduce whatever else you want but don't mess with "like."

Though Rath was never on record as having said so himself. There were many areas where he declined to say what he thought. And these included what he had begun to think of as Charley's project, even as he knew she wanted it to be their project and their way out and their reconciliation with whatever could be reconciled. Yet he couldn't quite accept it as even halfway his. If it was halfway his, he should believe in it more. Did the fact they were both paying for it make it theirs? Did the fact the whole town thought it was theirs make it theirs? Walter had always bent to his son's arguments, for being the arguments of youth itself, like spring water and who could argue with spring water as it bubbled out of the ground? But with Stephen's loss, it was harder to remember the gurgle. Was this where the Land of Cockaigne entered? It was a critique, as Brueghel's painting was a critique. It pained him to think that his son had come up with a ridiculous idea.

Though he didn't believe that either, and it was only a way to let off steam. What did he think, then? People usually ask themselves this question when their minds are far away and they're

28

calling to them to come home for dinner. Rath had said that to somebody once, then hated his oracular streak—or was it better to call it plain precious? The Land of Cockaigne: why not just buy a load of heroin off the boat? There was so much Rath didn't believe. And Charley, with her well-meaningness and hurt? Charley, Charley, Charley, he'd always liked the name, though there'd been a perfume once and maybe there still was, it was spelled with an "ie" so you couldn't blame it on her. Win one for the Gipper, that too.

On the day of the selectmen's meeting, he could hardly have been more unprepared. If you don't know what you're going to do, nobody else can know either, another of those axioms that came out of nowhere and forgot to leave Walter Rath's mind. The three-day rain was still coming and he'd patched his umbrella with a Band-Aid and walked the three blocks to the meeting, putting the umbrella against the wind. There would be the customary complaints that the power had gone off in the storm and couldn't the power company trim the trees for once before it was too late and about the transfer station where Phil Cummings was in rehab again for OxyContin and the girl they got in his place didn't know a milk carton from a hand grenade, but aside from this usual flotsam Rath knew from the stream of headlights lining up to park on State Street that Topic A would be the camp, and that it wouldn't be its supporters who turned out. There wasn't a floorboard in the town hall that didn't creak and he couldn't enter without a fuss. People were bringing in the folding chairs because the crowd would be that big and the meeting long and there was enough gray hair in the meeting and no one wanted to stand.

It was a selectmen's board of three. It had once been five but due to a shortage of candidates it had more recently been three. It was said people didn't want the job because it meant they couldn't go to Florida in January or had to fly back all the time at personal expense, but Rath didn't care about Florida and for him it was still an honor, being from away and for other reasons also. Rath held Sneeds Harbor in his republican dreams even if he kept that part of it a secret.

As he imagined, once finances were out of the way the first order of business was the transfer station and the second the residues of the storm, which meant it was forty-five minutes before Herbert Fallows stood and raised his hand at the same time and asked if Walter in particular could inform the town, in his official capacity or otherwise, what the truth was to the stories going around of a development out at the old Whitlock camp. The Whitlocks were the family that had built the resort in the woods a century previous and started the summer camp in the Thirties, and they were a Sneeds family that went back, and people in Sneeds in general referred to a place by its oldest known name, which had a way of keeping things in perspective. Rath understood the larger implication, too, that the place wasn't entirely his and Charley's to do whatever in the world they wanted with—maybe they had the legal right but not a moral one, there were ancestors to consider, as if it were a native burial ground. Rath understood this larger implication as it was something he had considered, and while it might have been a great surprise to others, it was less so to himself that he agreed with it more than he didn't. He could see the ancestors out in the woods and he could see himself who had come from nowhere and there were things that seemed more fair than money. Though he had not said any of it to Charley. And he could see the other side, too, for want of a better way to put it the "Charley side," that there would be nothing ever gained in life if only dead hands ruled. So it was at best a seventy-thirty thing, or a sixty-forty thing, something you put numbers to even if the numbers didn't quite add up. And if they didn't add up, then wasn't a decent regard for the other the only way left? He hadn't said that to Charley either, or if he ever had, it was before Stephen had gone out to the market for garlic at night.

The selectmen sat at bridge tables at the front of the room and there was a whiteboard in back of them and fluorescent lights above but at least their chairs didn't fold up but rather were sturdy old wooden swivel chairs with arms. Walter wore a chamois shirt that night and khakis and a two-day beard, camouflage in a way, though if it was camouflage he had worn it so long it almost announced "Walter Rath" when he walked in the room. He kept a thoughtful pose a couple of seconds and ran his tongue over his teeth, then he began with the first-person plural, which felt like the original sin of it all. "Herbert, there is something, but we've been waiting to see if it was real or not."

He went on for about ten minutes and he told more than he hid. The Bronx, the program, Sharon, the bids to fix up the camp. There weren't many secrets, anyway, as it was locals in most of the cases who had put in the bids. What Rath did keep secret from the room was how much he agreed with Fallows's implication, as if he could almost see old man Whitlock in the back of the town hall room. It was a room with tall windows and a tin ceiling and Walter felt its old rectangularity as if it were keeping his mind on track. He would secretly agree, more or less, with everything people had been saying behind their backs for weeks and would say now to his face, but they would never know his secret because there was Charley too to consider, and the possibility as well that she was right and he was wrong, and they would honor their son after all.

So Maggie Lassiter brought up her long-standing concern that it was a long way for these children from New York to come and that it would be better for *them*, mind you, to stay a bit closer to home, though Maggie appreciated everything that Walter and Charley had done for the community and their generosity which was on full display with this whole idea of theirs. Walter replied that first of all it wasn't *their* idea, but Stephen's, and secondly that the participants wouldn't really be children, these would be young men seventeen-to-nineteen years of age and wouldn't it be wonderful for them to see a little more of the world, and Sneeds Harbor's beautiful nature, and the whole idea that inspired Stephen was that they would experience the pleasures and richness and freedom that he himself and others in Sneeds had grown up with. They were under so much pressure in the city, from poverty and police and the street corner, always bearing down, and never being thought good enough, and it had been Stephen's idea that the farther away from all of that they could get, the better it would be.

Maggie was a persistent one and said she could see Stephen's point but she still couldn't believe there weren't woods and so on in parts of New York, she had a cousin in Oneonta, New York, and there were definitely woods there. Walter said she was correct, of course there were woods in New York state, but the Raths lived in Sneeds and Stephen had grown up in Sneeds and Sneeds was what inspired him and what he felt he had in him to share and so his parents would like to honor that.

Maggie could see that she wasn't going to get any further and that Walter was a good arguer, which in point of fact she already knew, so next up was the postmaster Carl Drummond who wasn't going to beat about the bush and frankly, he said, what he was concerned about was the same thing a lot of people were, which was the crime, in that it must be obvious that every one of these juvenile delinquents had already committed their share. In the spirit of candor and fair-mindedness, however, Bob Pearce put in that he'd now finished checking with the appropriate authorities in New York and there would be no murderers coming up, or at least none who'd been caught as murderers, though there could of course be no guarantee that there wouldn't be an individual among these persons who'd committed a murder and hadn't been caught for it. Walter thanked Bob for the conscientious research he'd undertaken, but wanted everyone to know that none of the participants, none, would have been convicted of murder or robbery or rape or even the first degree of assault. As for other crimes, the kids would be out at the camp most of the time and would know full well that one slip-up could mean their being sent home, so that while people would understand there could be no guarantees, still, he, Walter, felt that any crime, if it occurred, would be the exception to the rule and minor, and, yes, it was taking a small chance, but he knew the generous spirit of the town, and was confident that the small risk was worth taking.

And so it went on for about an hour and a half, the interrogation of Walter Rath and his rebuttals and defenses. Cal Bowden wanted to know about drug use, and would they be bringing drugs into the village. Richard Hammond, the lobsterman with the biggest boat in town, expressed the view that unfortunately once you start giving people pleasures no questions asked, they get addicted to them and only want more, so they're never satisfied and you can make matters worse, which was a lesson you could learn from lobstering, where you could hardly get a decent sternman who wasn't using something these days. Two or three people brought up the subject of real-estate values. Dot Corbin puzzled the room, as she often did, by asking if these boys would know how to swim, but then clarified, so that at least her point was understood, by asking would the town be liable if one drowned.

There wasn't one of these opinions, even those like Dot's which gathered a few snickers in the back rows, that Walter Rath didn't see some point to. It may have been no more than his nature to see the two sides of every coin even while the coin was being flipped in the air. But it was also his love of the town speaking, or rather, not speaking aloud but screaming in his mind, even as he gently batted down one objection after another, laid concerns to rest, and prepared his neighbors for the inevitable.

No one the whole night mentioned the words color or race or Black or white. They knew enough about the world not to. The rain had settled into a spray when Rath walked his few blocks home. He put his umbrella away and let his face and hair get wet. He was thinking he would make Charley happy by telling her how he had stuck up for their plan.

An Email Walter Received Before Going in
the Rain to the Selectmen's Meeting

Frank Symonson

Re: Saving the World

To: Walter Rath

Hey Walter—Thought you'd want to see this. I know, I know, it could sound like a lot of kumbaya, but it wasn't, it was serious shit. Some of the best forward-thinking minds in the country meeting in Vermont to see where we are and where we have to get to. The topics (and I quote): "*poverty, inequality, human rights, the climate crisis, racism, war, peace, refugees, workers, healthcare, housing, civil rights, independent media, corporate power, criminal justice reform, international solidarity, voting rights, the rights of women, the LGBTQ community, immigration, democracy, economics, politics, organizing, and ultimately how all of these issues can never be adequately addressed in isolation.*" Please, I'm not kidding, there's a video, link below, check it out. F.

Oh Frank, oh Frank, was something of what Rath thought when he read the litany of ills that would be solved at once or not at all. Then a little while later, walking in the rain, he thought: Frank could probably use a job.

Frank was Walter's friend back at Yale where everyone admired Frank and wanted to be his friend for being at the top of the greased pole, right schools, right family, right '48 Indian, but Walter really was his friend, the kid from Grand Rapids and the kid from Oyster Bay. They'd been suitemates, too, junior and senior years, and Frank had been the one who found the Brueghel on the street. Then later it was said Frank had gone off one deep end or the other, though Walter himself had never been sure. Once ahead of the curve, always ahead of the curve, and you could get so far ahead that people where you'd left them behind couldn't see you anymore. That was one theory of the case, the other being that Frank had taken the easy way, the stoner-in-absentia halfway off the grid and halfway out of his mind. Now he lived inland and somewhat west in a cabin in the woods in a town made famous for Sandy Koufax having lived there a little while when he was retired and trying to escape the world his left arm had given him. *Frank could use a job.* Rath thought of it a couple of times more before entering the town hall, and thought as well of Frank being the one who had found *The Land of Cockaigne* on the street, then he didn't think of Frank again until later.

It Had to be You

They were crosswise to each other on the bed and he was rubbing her feet. How'd it go she'd wanted to know and he was telling her, of Maggie and Harold and Cal and the rest, a smile or two for Dot. He said nothing about his own reservations and if you'd asked him why, he might have said that he was waiting, because Rath was one who believed that you will know the time to say something when it falls out of your mouth, the words unbidden and bare. Rehearsed words gave themselves away, he felt, or perhaps it was only he wasn't actor enough to pull them off. As for her feet, they were a little cold and he warmed them.

They were often quiet with each other these evenings. It seemed less profane. So many odd thoughts seemed profane, making their claims or showing off. There was still the business of life, of course. In daylight they did all the business of life, and they would catch each other up. As for the rest, the little asides, the endearments, the ornaments, who could say when they would come back, like the spring birds or not at all.

They streamed old movies too, but not this night. After he'd told her everything that was easy to tell the only parts left were those that might wound her or him or them both depending how it went and she could startle or resent or be surprised and turn unworldly quiet, like the quiet of the spheres when the music stopped, or decide as she sometimes did that he was too smart for his own good. They'd been down all those roads. Now it looked like she might fall asleep as her eyes had slowed and he could have let it pass to a tomorrow to be named later but, as if mostly to be perverse, a few words he'd not known were there presented themselves, volunteers for a dangerous mission that needed but a few good men, so that he was left with no choice but to say, "I wonder sometimes," then he stopped.

She was awake now and she curled the blanket closer to her chin. It pulled away from her feet and he let her feet go. She pulled her knees up, too, so that she was closer to a ball.

"Wonder what?" she asked.

"How Stephen really thought about this thing," Walter said.

"Are you starting something?" she said.

"I guess I am," he said.

"So you are," she said.

He paused as if to let air or light or something into the room where they lay. She pulled on the blanket to tighten it around her.

"I was only trying to imagine it. I can hear his laughter. With his first thought of it. It was almost a lark, a screwball idea, a what-if."

"And if it was?"

"Then maybe we're taking the whole thing too seriously."

"You mean I am," she said.

"We both are," he said.

"You needn't be chivalrous," she said.

"I'll be chivalrous if I want," he said.

"Why do you hate this project?" she said.

"I don't hate it," he said.

"Then what?" she said.

"I just don't entirely feel Stephen in it," he said.

Now it seemed to Charley that they were getting somewhere, and she unballed herself a little and said with still an edge but a different one, "You mean you don't feel yourself in it. You're embarrassed by it. Or by him, by Stephen?"

"Of course not."

"Then what the hell, Walter? Do you think it won't work? Is that it?"

"It may not," he said.

"Of course it may not," she said.

"I do have doubts," he said.

"That's obvious," she said.

"One, they'll be bored."

"And two?"

"Two, they'll be bored."

"Anything else?"

"Yeah. It doesn't feel super-neighborly."

"Oh my God!"

"It's why, when I imagined him having this idea, I saw him being only half serious. You know how much he loved this place."

"That's exactly why, don't you see?"

"Maybe," he said.

"He *wanted* this, Walter. He talked about it with Sharon. A *lot*. It wasn't just some one-time thing."

"You never told me that."

"You think I'm making it up now? You think I'm lying?"

"No, but you never told me that."

"You do think I'm lying."

"Stop."

"You know what? I don't care if he laughed or he cried or he sneezed when he thought of it! And I don't care if it's 'super-neighborly,' either."

"Maybe people sense that."

"So you're going to blame it all on me? Go ahead, tell them it's your bitch wife, it's all her fault."

"Please, could we?"

"You're so afraid of what everybody's going to think. Oh, Walter Rath, the great wise man! The great savior! The local messiah, every town's got to have one!"

"Getting to be a boring conversation, Charley."

"You don't want to do this? You want to call it all off? No, you know what, I almost said that. No. We're not calling anything off."

"Of course we're not," he said.

It hardly broke a world record for their fights, but it was a pretty good one in Rath's estimation. There'd been almost a drought of their fights while they had so much to grieve. The rain was welcome in a way, assurance that the conditions of life had not changed.

That night a dream he had or the fragments of it he remembered were complicated. He was having an affair with someone or he wasn't and he didn't know with who, but he left the storage bin where they had stayed and there was Charley in a sun dress or a sunny dress as if no one could ever be sunnier with her teeth that were a little big and her smile that was a little afraid and in retreat and there was Charley caressing a wounded animal which was unlike any animal Walter had seen but she seemed to care for it regardless that its snout when he saw it at her breast was ugly and mean and there was Charley naked and long lying on a chaise and reaching in surprise for a towel because a Mexican boy in Oaxaca walked by, and Charley in a long winter coat walking somewhere in the snow but who could say where she was going because she seemed not to know herself, she was in a daze induced by life itself. And what Walter thought in his dream was *it had to be her* because for a few moments which were not from a dream but from life she had been more perfect to his need than any woman he had seen and he had seen a few, and so all the rest of the detritus of their lives of thirty years didn't matter, they could

40

fight till kingdom come and still it wouldn't matter, and when he went back to the storage bin in shame and longing it was she who was there.

The Caretaker

There wasn't a bar in Sneeds Harbor and the nearest was the Canterbury up on Route One and it was there that Donnie Cormer met Rine Worsley after the selectmen's meeting was done. Rine was one of those identified by Doris Bunting as never having been farther than Bangor and he was all in all proud of it. He had six generations before him who had gotten by right where they were except to go fight in the wars and he didn't see the point of anything different, a supposed set of facts which he would bore you with apropos of usually not much, though in his defense there were sometimes ironic whiffs in his telling, as if to admit if somebody had struck the lottery things might have gone differently. Rine did roadwork for the state in the season and he went back five decades with Donnie, to a time when the school had been full.

They were two men too wide for the stools they were sitting on, from the door resembling twins of wear and experience. Donnie had been filling Rine in on the selectmen's meeting, as Rine had been over at the Eastern Maine hospital with his wife and her diabetes complications. Rine shook his head several times and kept his counsel while Donnie listed his own concerns, which he had not given voice to at the meeting, for the reason that he'd taken care of the Raths' places since they came to Sneeds, which was more than two decades, and they'd always been decent, around the holidays of course but in general. The concerns Donnie cited weren't strikingly different from those expressed by others, that these kids they were inviting up could be troublemakers, that people liked Sneeds for its peace and quiet, that if you could live with a little economic uncertainty the village was fine just the way it was, and that while it welcomed newcomers, with the Raths being a prime example of the red carpet rolled out, the newcomers ought to take some care and respect the village's feelings, which were definitely mixed, to say the least of it. He added that from what he could tell the whole state had hardly any Black people at all but when you looked at the pictures in the Bangor paper of who was arrested for crimes, half of them were Black.

Of course that was the case, Rine confirmed, picking at the label of his third PBR. It was even worse than that probably, because people in the government didn't want you to know about it so half the time they didn't even put the pictures in.

Donnie wasn't agreed on that last observation, because there were certainly enough pictures in the Bangor paper every time there was a crime solved, but he took Rine's basic point, about the government not wanting you to know things.

Then Rine wanted to hear about the zoning and if it came up in the meeting. "Change the zoning, that's how you stop it," he said.

But Donnie said it had come up and unfortunately with the way the bylaws worked you had to put new zoning to a vote, which meant it couldn't be soon enough.

"See, there is the entire problem, right there," Rine said. "You can't get anything done. Everything you try to do, you can't do."

"Amen to that," Donnie said.

"And I'll tell you something else they don't talk about, I'll wager dollars to dimes. They say anything about next year?"

"No. Just the summer, that's all they're talking about."

"Because they want to sneak it in, and once these kids are up, you think they'll leave? Oh, sure, they'll call home to get more drugs." Rine tongued the nipple of his beer bottle in case the joke should be missed. "No, my point is ... I mean, sure, they'll go home, *that* bunch'll go ... but what about next year? Once it gets started, it'll be forever, and bigger and bigger, they just don't want to say so."

"To get the precedent established," Donnie concurred, though until this moment that part of it hadn't much occurred to him.

"To get the precedent established, precisely," Rine said, then looked along the bar to see who might be in hearing range, which really wasn't anybody, it being late on a slow night.

"You know I've been educating myself lately," he said, more sternly.

But his tone as much as his words got a laugh out of Donnie, who had a quick and hiccupy laugh. "That'd be a new one."

"The way they're always telling everybody the whole internet's a pack of lies? Well, they say that so you won't find the ones that aren't lies."

"I can't be bothered," Donnie said. "Play a few games, go to sleep."

"Hey, nobody's stopping you, but I'm telling you, my friend, it's out there, you just gotta go find it. You think this Rath thing, it's just about a few so-called African-Americans?"

Rine had lowered his voice, though even the bartender was way down the bar.

"Don't go nutjob on me now, would you, please?" Donnie said, which from long experience of Rine he knew to be a possibility.

"Okay, pal, zip my mouth. I say no more."

"You are some asshole, Rine."

"You want me to tell you what my research uncovered or not?"

"Lord Jesus! ... Sure. What?"

Rine got his phone out. "Here. Black and white. You don't have to believe me, read for yourself."

But there were no bars of reception in the bar. "Fuck it. Okay." He squeezed the phone back into his jeans.

"What would you guess, where would you guess, Walter Rath comes from?"

"Michigan."

"Yeah, but ethnicity. Nationality. What I'm saying, we got a socialistic plot right here in River City. It could be a small part of the enchilada, but it's definitely a part, one more part, and they get enough parts together and that'll be the ball game. You know who Karl Marx was, Donnie?"

"No."

"Karl Marx was the whole inventor of communism, and he was … a Jew. And his best buddy, Trotsky, who implemented it for him? … Jew. And Walter Rath? … Jew."

It was dark in the bar but Rine's eyes seemed to catch a bit of fire, to match the glow of the hidden jewel he'd just revealed.

"I knew Mr. Rath was Jewish. He told me two or three times. She isn't, you know."

"She could be by proximity."

"You know, until this camp thing came up, I couldn't say one bad thing about them," Donnie said. "And they lost their kid. Nice kid, grew up with Kev."

"I'm only talking about the guy, anyway. Race-mixing is what their goal is. Which they plan to continue until the white man is so reduced he won't know if he's coming or going. He hardly *will be* the white man anymore. There won't be a one of us left. That's their goal."

"Mr. Rath's goal?"

"Let's just say, maybe he can't help it, it's by blood."

"I don't believe it," Donnie said.

"Suit yourself," Rine said. "You heard it here first."

"If you ask me, it's more her thing anyway. All I see is her doing the work."

"And all I'm going to say, hers, his, one or the other, I'm not going to allow it to happen. It's not happening on my watch."

"What are you going to do?"

"Unh-uh. Unh-uh. You're not a good enough comrade for me to tell you."

It was pretty much the end of that part of the conversation. Donnie didn't know what to say after that and when they started talking again it was about a new snowplow for Donnie's truck that he had seen when he was over in Ellsworth reduced by several hundred dollars and he wanted to know if Rine knew anything about it, which he didn't but said he'd look into it and recommended to Donnie that he read the reviews online. Rine wasn't always off the deep end, Donnie thought, and it was a shame when he was but wasn't it also the case that stopped clocks are right twice a day, which was something Donnie felt could also be applied to Rine.

At home, Donnie was still thinking about Rine. He pissed him off. He was arrogant and cocksure and by what right was that? But this whole socialistic plot thing bothered Donnie. After all, there were enough signs of it going around. You could almost say it got the president elected, in a reverse kind of way. As for the Jews, Donnie didn't know that they were involved with all that. Mr. Rath certainly didn't seem to be. On the other hand, this whole camp idea was a wound. The Raths should have talked to him before they came out with it. That's what it came down to. They'd often consulted with him in the past when they knew Sneeds less well and needed to know one thing or the other and when had he ever steered them wrong? Never, would be the answer in Donnie's view. So could it be this new socialist thing had secretly brainwashed their minds? Donnie could remember plenty of movies where minds got stolen and it seemed ridiculous for it to happen in real life but what if? There was too much going on in the world for a guy like himself to be on top of all of it. He admitted this to himself. Just as a mental calculation, as Caryn lay asleep beside him, he totted up how much money he received from the Raths each year, which he would have to replace if he went and quit. It was quite a sum.

Fifteen Hours in the Bronx

At 7:07 a.m. she opened her eyes to a day the Lord hath made which was what her mama always said so who was she to put the words out of her mind? The words clung to the bed frame and squinted with her eyes and came through the dirty panes in streaks of unexpected sorrow.

At 8:17 she was on the Grand Concourse because it was a walk to work, with the heat of early summer already up and men brushing by her and her mind clogged with the day.

At 9:03 she finished the *Times* and left it on a colleague's desk because they passed one copy around, then checked her email but there was nothing there that she was looking for.

At 9:31 there was Tyrell who had a thin face and a stutter which she found charming and he'd been a P in the program after boosting scooters with some others, which wasn't much and wasn't his idea, though she might have liked him better if it was or at least if he said it was, because the other had all the chances of a lie. Tyrell, she said, I've done a whole lot of these interviews so tell me something new, and he said he'd always wanted to see a Christmas tree that was growing in the ground and wasn't just laying on the sidewalk waiting to get bought like a slave, all of which he said with his stutter, which was enough for her and she put him in the pile that said yes.

At 10:03 there was Markus who was nineteen and big all around who'd mistaken an AI computer for an air conditioner when he stole it out of the back of a van, thought AI was AC, he said, and she laughed and looked at her sheet that showed he had no family at all, which she asked him about and which he confirmed, he lived sometimes in an SRO and sometimes on the street, and she put him in the yes pile, so that now she had thirteen and needed but two more.

At 10:50 there was Manuel who was late and lied about it, a cat-ate-the-homework kind of lie that she sighed a tired sigh to hear and put him in the pile that said no.

At 11:03 for no reason she could figure except that the next kid hadn't arrived or she was flying up there tomorrow but anyway she thought of Stephen and it was like Stephen Stephen Stephen all Stephen all the time for two or three minutes that seemed longer, her mind adrift in what-ifs and half-forgotten glory.

At 11:07 she checked her email again and there was nothing there that she was looking for.

At 11:15 there was Luis who wore wing-tipped shoes to the interview and was rather proud of knowing who Almodóvar was and having watched *Volver* on his phone, and may have been muling crack on his block only to try to prove to himself that he was someone he wasn't, which was a sentiment that Sharon could appreciate, and she had her fourteenth boy.

At 12:17 p.m. she sat at her desk with her lunch of cottage cheese and mango and fruity water and considered whether, having checked her messages as many times as she'd checked them and found nothing there that she was looking for, she might just give them a call at the Overworld Theatre Company in the Methodist church on Avenue C to see if they'd had a chance to look at her presentation and if so, what they thought. She considered the odds of whether it would be obnoxious or too soon or would anyone even be there now and if they weren't or they didn't pick up, should she leave a message?

At 12:25 she began dialing the number she had for the

Overworld Theatre Company but she stopped at the last digit as if afraid to launch a rocket to the moon and put her phone face down on her desk to keep temptation away.

At 2:30 there was Antwan who pleaded with her to get him out of town because he had six sisters if you included the halves and he was afraid of himself, that if they didn't get money soon he would put the oldest of them on the street, but if he was out of town he couldn't do that, could he? It was another story she didn't believe and hated it as well and put him on the pile that said no.

At 3:08 there was Rigoberto who had a nice crooked smile and said he was the king of fare-beaters, there was no better fare-beater in the South Bronx, he never paid for a ride and he was proud of it and even prouder of the hundreds he'd held the gate for. She no longer took the train so much but having lived half the years of her life on Manhattan Avenue it was an impulse she could understand and she liked the smile that was so without pretense and she had her fifteenth boy.

At 3:52, having spent half an hour going through her notes for gang affiliations and the like to be sure there were no obvious conflicts, she phoned Charley to tell her she had her kids, eight African-American boys and seven Hispanic boys and something she liked in each of them, and they talked about the plane and Charley said she'd be there to get her.

At 4:06 she was still at her desk and reasoned that if anybody was going to pick up at the Overworld Theatre Company number it would be after lunch but before the evening curtain and it had been fifteen days and they said they'd get right back to her and what could it hurt to show how much she cared? So she dialed and got the voice mail of Andrea Birnbaum whom she knew to be the founder and artistic director, which only made sense now that she heard the voice since how could this theatre that met in a church on Avenue C afford its own phone, but because it was the artistic director she had a moment's panic and forgot what to say and nearly hung up but didn't because Andrea would now have her number and think her a coward or worse, so she said to the voice mail, "Hi. This is Sharon Mason. I left my directing portfolio with you a couple of weeks ago, applying for an internship? Just wondering if you'd had a chance to look at it. No rush, but when you can, please call."

At 5:26, with the courthouse closed and no more boys to be interviewed and not having heard from Andrea Birnbaum by phone or email or text, all of which she checked, she left her desk and soon, by 5:32, was walking on the Concourse again on a city afternoon of sweat and cloud thinking what a fool she'd been to call and what a needy, pathetic message she'd left, with the upspeak and all of it.

At 6:17 she got her mail from her mailbox but there was nothing there that she was looking for.

At 6:41 she opened her fridge to think of dinner and thought instead of the head of garlic that Stephen didn't have; and she thought also if they hadn't made love so much or if the bodega had been open late or if she had insisted that he not go out of the apartment at ten-thirty at night and leave her there to wonder.

At 7:43 she ate dinner alone at the table that had room for two but only one chair and watched whichever leftie newsers happened to be on and rued the state of the nation in what she knew to be her pious half hour.

At 7:52 she washed her dishes.

At 8:18 she finished packing for tomorrow.

At 8:31 she checked her email and there was an email from Andrea Birnbaum that had just come in and what it said was unfortunately they had no place in their internship program at the present time but please keep in touch, so that was that, so that was that.

At 8:32 she rued her lack of talent and wondered why she ever thought she had a chance.

At 8:47 as if in penance for her foolishness she paid bills, Verizon, Con Ed, the cable, the MasterCard. There was also an envelope from Mount Holyoke College that had been sitting there for months quietly asking to be remembered like a cat that turns its face to you every time you enter a room and she filled it with a fifty-dollar check and kissed it shut.

At 8:52 as she washed her face and brushed her teeth she wondered if she would have done better if she'd gone to Bard, where all the theatre kids went, or Bennington, either one, but Mount Holyoke had given her the scholarships in her need. And anyway it was years past now and if she had the talent it would have shown through, so don't go making excuses, girl, or you'll soon sound like one of your Ps.

At 9:41, having read a little, she set her alarm for five because she'd have to be in an Uber to LaGuardia by six.

At 9:48 she entered into a dreamless sleep.

Friends

There had been a road to the hotel in the woods and the Raths had found its traces and restored it and maintained it for a fire road and it was this road that Charley and Sharon followed into the woods, slathered with natural repellents that Charley bought online from a sketchy purveyor in the Berkshires and with their pants tucked into their socks against the ticks. The woods were spruce and fir and larch but mostly spruce, and these too the Raths maintained, so that when the women got to where the Nazareth had stood before it burned, they could see thirty feet in to the foundations and the shards of walls. It had been called the Nazareth because Hiram Whitlock had traveled in the Holy Land and the name was both a remembrance and a brag, but it burned after five years. "We decided not to clear it," Charley told her. "Walter loves the traces of things."

They had already talked business and discussed plans and inspected the basketball court in progress that Sharon had proposed as insurance for the homesick and that Charley had deemed a marvelous idea and they'd talked as well about Sharon's flight up and the weather and Bronx Cares and where Sharon grew up and where Charley grew up and more, so that Charley had decided that Sharon was thoughtful and efficient and even possibly a little bit kind and her new friend and Sharon had decided that Charley seemed to need a friend and in general seemed to have needs greater than her own, but why not and who could say and it didn't really matter so she would be her friend if she needed one. When

Charley said, "Walter loves the traces of things," Sharon imagined him, whom she'd met only that once in New York, as an archaeologist in a pith hat and here were his ruins.

Charley asked her if she wanted to go in and they tiptoed over brush and broken logs to get closer. Bricks littered the wet humus. Two bathtubs, as if the last things anyone wanted, lay upside down at angles to each other, their claw feet up in the air. Pieces of wall, overgrown with rotted stumps, rose two feet or three and disappeared in forest darkness. A chimney, a crushed fireplace, a sink with its drain pipe still attached. It was as if something had been built without a plan. And yet there was poignancy in just the opposite: that there had been a plan and it failed. The morning sunlight went only so far. Charley wanted to tell her how this was the place where the ten Black people had worked but she remembered that she had already told her that story. There was nowhere to sit and their socks were soaking through from the humus underfoot and they would have left then but Sharon thought to say what she had been thinking since she got off the plane. "You want to hear something sort of funny? Not funny, interesting. *Interesting.* This is really going to happen, isn't it? I mean, we're this far. I saw the hoops going up on the court, I thought, it's kind of amazing, to build something where there was nothing, just an idea. It's important not to get blasé about that, isn't it?"

"It is," Charley said.

"But, you know, when this started, it was a joke. Stephen said to me, he even said, wouldn't it be funny if."

"If what?" Charley said.

"Just this. If we brought all these kids, our program kids, up here, where they hadn't seen a Black person in a hundred years."

"He said it as a joke?" Charley said.

"Of course, after that, we got serious. We really meant it."

She was staring just then at the two upside-down bathtubs.

Charley followed Sharon's gaze and for the flash of an eye hated herself for hating Walter for always being right. In the shafts of the forest sun the porcelain of the old tubs still gleamed white, so that they looked like dogs waiting for their bellies to be scratched.

Rose Britton was eighty-six and had been eating lunch on the patio outside the Historical Society for fifty years give or take and so that was where Charley and Sharon met her. Charley could have done without the patio, which was appended to the one institution in Sneeds that wore its respectability on its sleeve, but she loved Rose, who drove around Sneeds in an old Mercedes coupe with the top down. It had been her husband's Mercedes coupe and he had lavished money and sweat and endless patience on it with the result that when he died it felt like the thing that could keep him closest to her. Ward Britton had been prominent in the State Department under Kennedy and Johnson and taken a fall for Vietnam but landed at Princeton and Rose had been aboard for all of it, along the way coming to know the world well and in her own right had translated Verlaine. So Charley wanted her old friend to meet her new friend. Not entirely unlike the Raths, the Brittons had come to Sneeds Harbor because nobody else they knew did. Their friends tended to be over in Northeast, or elsewhere on Mount Desert. The friends, those who were still alive, seldom ventured as far as Sneeds these days and Rose led a somewhat lonely if cantankerous life, reading and driving around. The day had clouded over. There was a southwest breeze that promised more of the same. Rose had brought a thermos of lime rickeys. The little café inside turned out a passing BLT club. Charley had told Sharon she wasn't fond of the patio and this had reassured Sharon but when she saw two middle-aged women in skorts come out of the Historical Society she wished she were back in the woods. The saving grace was that Rose Britton dressed in polka dots and didn't care.

For a half hour they had the sort of lunch where every topic of consequence was avoided but this was only because Rose was just warming up. Sharon didn't know what to make of her, whether she was a parody or for real or wise enough to be both. She spoke with the authority of the Episcopalian who assumes the right to rule yet with a wink that says who cares. They talked about the weather and lime rickeys and whether Riverdale was really the Bronx or should secede and about the handful of ignorant, deplorable people around Sneeds who were rumored to be petitioning the Bureau of Motor Vehicles to get Rose's drivers license revoked. Then she said, as if a dinner bell had been rung, "Now tell me."

Charley and Sharon waited, but so did Rose. She declined to elaborate, forcing Charley finally to ask the obvious. "Tell you …"

"Well, what's going on. I want the dirty. Quite honestly, I don't know what you're doing. Of course I *know*, you've told me, but what's the point of it all, what's the attitude? I suppose that's it, the attitude."

These were the sorts of things Charley was accustomed to Rose saying, asking about attitude when the attitude was mostly hers. It was also among the many aspects of Rose she was fond of, her gimlet-eyed defiance. "We're just trying to do something to sweeten the lives of a few kids," she began. "They've all been screwed by something, whether it's upbringing or poverty or the justice system. Give 'em a break for a change."

Sharon wasn't sure it was her place but she said anyway, more as if she were supplying information than making an argument, "All the programs around, mine included, they always *expect* something from them, to behave, to pay attention, to learn or earn or be warned about something."

"No obligations for two weeks. Just show up," Charley said.

"Nobody ever treats these kids generously, as if they were special. But what happens if you try that?" Sharon said.

"Except no drugs," Charley said.

"And no girls," Sharon said.

"Just good food, sleep late, the woods, the water, nature," Charley said.

"And basketball," Sharon said.

"When I first told Walter, he called it the Land of Cockaigne."

It was a little bit of a barrage, a self-conscious defense, as if the older woman's original question in its earnestness had caught them by surprise, and weren't they supposed to know what they were doing and why?

Rose kept nodding in uncertain agreement but then she brightened. "The Land of Cockaigne? With no one getting laid?" The obviousness of the problem, of the misattribution if you will, served to focus the skepticism she'd felt from the start. "You see, this is what I don't understand. Is it moral education? Or something more sybaritic? Exposing them to the so-called best things in life, or to the things they want? Showing them how the other half lives to enrich them or make them envious? It all seems wobbly to me. I love you, Charley, but you need to be clear."

"Well, certainly not that, certainly not envious," Charley finally said.

"But why not? It might goad them into action, into doing more with their lives," Rose said.

"We're trying to make this nice," Charley said.

"Nice? That's your whole problem, *nice*. You're too nice, everyone's too nice. Don't you see what I'm saying, dears?"

Perhaps they did or perhaps they didn't, Rose having, in Charley's opinion, her own oracular way of being less than clear. But Charley let it go with a nod. She didn't want to ruin Sharon's afternoon. She didn't want her to fear the contingency in any of it. Rose could see the plight of her friend and that she herself had plunged in as deep as the wound could bear, and went back to fretting aloud about her drivers license. They couldn't take it away for a few minor mishaps, could they? She would have to hire a lawyer. My God, the painful, stupid expense. Charley and Sharon were left to wonder.

Walter was surprised to hear that Frank was coming down. They had talked about him coming down but had not got around to a date or a plan, which was another thing Walter liked about Frank, that they could talk in generalities and then Frank would just show up. It was proof, in a way, that you couldn't beat the world with better organization. Charley's organizational skills, while admirable, wore Walter down. It wasn't that Walter was anti-organization, but he was anti-too-much-organization, and Frank was living proof that you could get by otherwise. But he still wanted to get him a job. So how much luck was it that on the very day Sharon Mason was around, Frank was getting his teeth cleaned in Bar Harbor. Sneeds was less than an hour.

Frank was always late, so that when he said he would be there by three, Walter expected him at four. By then something was brewing in the southwest sky that promised more than the early breeze. Walter loved to see Frank riding his old Ducati down the road, his red-gray beard like a pirate, his saddle bags filled with the flotsam of a man living alone. He was a secret admirer of Frank's freedom, the more so because he knew it was chosen. Frank could have been most things, a lawyer, a banker, a gentleman farmer, a genial academic in a field all his own, or maybe an arctic explorer or CIA comer, a guy destined to rise, but he had chosen this. Or he seemed to have chosen it, though it was possible as well that after awhile it had snuck up on him. Walter waited outside the house to hear the motorcycle's throat. Charley and Sharon weren't back. Charley must still have been showing her around.

Frank always brought a little gift, too, a baguette or a bit of weed. This time it was a postcard he'd found in a thrift shop that showed America's imperialist reach. Walter greeted him with the remark that he didn't know Frank was so punctilious about getting his teeth cleaned. But actually he was, every three months (or the dentist said he'd lose them), and at considerable expense for a guy who got his internet by running a line off a pole. Frank's father had wound up at the top of the heap of Enron, but the company's fall had taken away the last of the son's safety nets. Frank was in a cheerful mood. He'd found a new candidate, a Hawaiian woman recently elected who was going to save the country from its morass, which in Frank's view began with Trump but certainly didn't end there.

And he was eager to talk about her, her anti-war views, her anti-banker views, her save-the-planet views. Walter got out a six-pack. For a stoner, Frank liked his beer. The two of them sat on the back porch and watched the darkening horizon. Frank's long legs pushed the porch swing in a pendulum motion as he spoke. He was a head taller than Walter yet these days weighed less by fifteen pounds. His feet were calloused, his sandals dangled, his cheeks were gaunt beneath the beard. Walter asked him if the Hawaiian woman had anything to do with the Vermont conference that Frank had sent him the email about. She didn't, Frank said, but had Walter looked at the video? It was really astonishingly good, it really said much of what had to be said, Frank said.

Walter confessed that he'd only looked at bits of it. And even those "bits" hedged the truth of how much he had actually seen. He'd fast-forwarded through the first five minutes. Frank encouraged him to go back to it. It was about intersectionality, Frank said, just as his Hawaiian woman was all about intersectionality.

But what *is* intersectionality, Walter wanted to know. It wasn't that he hadn't heard the word, but he wanted to hear from Frank what it was and how he understood it, as if it were some mystic secret that had to be transmitted mouth to ear. Frank drained his beer and began what he called his two-minute explanation. The two-minute explanation came to ten and Walter's eyes were blurring and he'd long since come to rue the comradely question that had gotten Frank going, but something in the ninth or tenth minute of it all caught his attention for the degree it sounded like Frank's email, the laundry list of the world's ills, so long that it might have been a contest or some obnoxious little intellectual game to see who could remember the largest number of them. Walter's grandmother on his mother's side had voted for the socialist Norman Thomas for president every chance she had, and he'd read *Kapital* front to back and Piketty and others and it wasn't that he couldn't see the wrongs. Nor was it that he rued the pessimism that could compose so long a list. On the contrary, listening to Frank, his old friend, deepened his own pessimism, it seemed to drive deeper each second Frank spoke, it drove even into Walter's soul if Walter could be said to have a soul, for that was another area that he was pessimistic about, man's possession of the old encrusted thing about which so much muck had been written. Or was it possible, he occasionally speculated, that man in general had a soul but that he, Walter, had been shortchanged in that department? He was not one to confide his darker thoughts to anyone, nor often enough even to himself, but Frank's too-naive pessimism, his evils that could all be fixed if like a flock of chickens they could just be wrestled into one big sack, turned him darker and, perhaps, even angry enough to speak. Frank was too fucking optimistic!

And Walter might still have held his tongue, but he had heard such spiels from Frank so often, and the world, and Frank, always stayed the same.

"Not sure I agree," Walter said.

"You've got to see the video," Frank said.

"I don't think it's got to do with the video. The video can't cover it," Walter said.

"One-by-one, two-by-two, I don't know," Frank said.

"It's not that, either," Walter said.

Frank had a moment where he imagined that Walter might have sustained a religious conversion, like you might sustain a concussion or something, but it was not that, either. There had been a subtle change in the barometric pressure. Or there might have been and it felt like it, then Walter's rage or carelessness or fatigue from hearing Frank's ideas one too many times and their echoes in so much else that he read and heard all the time now and argued and resisted and doubted and poked mental holes in, got the better of him. "I don't really believe in any of it," he said.

"Any of what?" Frank asked.

"Any of it. Anymore. Just trying to be honest with you, Frank. I used to. I really did. I used to believe in a lot of things."

Was Frank eyeing him so comprehensively over his red-gray beard out of curiosity or disappointment or fear? Maybe it was only that Frank was such an old, old friend, and if he stayed stopped up with Frank, would Walter not stay stopped up with everyone and forever? It would be an experiment in a way, an experiment in what he could get away with. Nor were a couple of beers enough to blame.

"Where to start?" Walter continued. "You really want to know? Progress, for one thing. How's that? For openers. Progress, the word progressive to describe a person, they're horseshit, a propaganda, nothing more. Things change, they don't progress. The only thing that progresses is a mind that realizes that nothing progresses, then that mind progresses, and if one mind progresses then I suppose you could say that the whole of humanity progresses infinitesimally and maybe it progresses even an infinitesimal amount more if that one mind realizes that it's not *nothing* that progresses but rather itself. So I'm already a liar. I don't believe in progress but there is progress, it's just not the progress of the pols and the opiners and it's in short supply and the supply isn't likely to grow." Walter was speaking in his low, sad voice, the one that others often noticed and sometimes remarked, that sounded like he was swimming in a deep, cloudy pool. "Let's see. What else might piss people off? What else can I be a liar about? Every word that's lost its tang, that started as a rallying cry and became a crutch, liberty, equality, fraternity, life, liberty, the pursuit of happiness, the whole political gamut, diversity, inclusiveness, democracy, there's a good one, why democracy, has the *demos* proved itself so adept, has it draped itself in honor, has it striven for justice, for mercy, for courage, for understanding? So there, I must be a liar again, because I seem to still approve of these, justice and mercy and courage and understanding and the striving for any and all of them and who am I to approve or disapprove anyway, who asked Walter Rath? Walter Rath the eternal Jew if you want to start getting serious about it. And what about love?"

Frank, of course, had expected none of this. Not from Walter the Wise, Walter the Circumspect, his old friend. "Do you believe in love?" he asked, a flanking move in a way.

But Walter couldn't help himself now. It was something that was simply happening, his response to the whole world that somehow Frank and his email and Charley's dedication and Sharon and their camp for the kids and the doubts of the town and the death of his son had brought to the doorstep of his mind. "I believe in love. It's belief itself I'm skeptical about, or rather those who too easily say they believe, in the political sphere, where people say it most easily of all, but possibly in all the spheres."

"So you've become a nihilist," Frank said in a sympathetic tone. "My old friend's become a nihilist."

"I'm neither an 'ist' nor an 'ism,'" Walter responded, "or at least I hope I'm not, yet probably deep down I am. Who can say? Who even knows enough of himself? Oh, that's another one, himself, herself, pronouns. 'Their!' They've got to be kidding, the 'theirs!' Going out of their way to make a mockery of the language, make it redolent of political convenience. That's another thing I think and never say. Why pick a fight with somebody? Why go to the trouble? Why have to think about it? And why trouble the downtrodden? You know why I came to this place, to Sneeds Harbor? Leaving Charley out of it for a moment, the chance we took for the marriage, for me it was a small, relatively isolated New England village with a lot of white houses that seemed to govern itself in the way of the original republic and the question would be, in my mind, or maybe rather the hope, that the original republic was all it was cracked up to be. So it was a test, in a way, an ongoing test. But it was the best test, and best hope, I could find. I loved it here. I still do. But do I believe myself when I say it? What a crock."

"At least you don't like yourself any better than you like the world," Frank said, still trying to be helpful, to provide some cushioning for what he took to be Walter's self-laceration.

"And yet I manage to go on, hypocrite that I am."

"Maybe we're all hypocrites," Frank said.

"We're all equal in that we live and we die," Walter said, sounding at last as if he were wearying of hearing himself and as if his audience would soon be gone. "We're unequal in a thousand other ways but the only way that counts is how we respond to those two facts. And who gets to grade those responses and is there a final exam? I hope God exists. Truly I do, to the extent I can be truthful about anything. But do I believe? All I believe is that faith will know if I'm faking."

"And I suppose you'd say about climate change and nuclear

winter that they're likely to cancel each other out?" Frank asked, referencing something he'd read in one of the Web's darker corners.

But Walter let that one pass. Tomorrow maybe he'd feel like a fool for popping off, but tomorrow was still a ways off. He looked out from the porch to see the storm coming in and was amused by it.

It was supposed to lay out in the Gulf but the storm took a turn and hit the land. There was driving hail in Bangor and trees fell and the power went off along the coast. Charley and Sharon were back at five-thirty, soaked and shivery and happy about it and looking in Charley's closet for something dry to wear. The flight from LaGuardia to Bangor had been canceled so there would be no plane at Bangor to fly back on. Sharon was marooned. Walter had earlier invited Frank to dinner, hoping to introduce him to Sharon on the fly and do something of an end run around Charley, who liked Frank well enough, and respected him for being Walter's longest friend, but had years of accumulated doubts about his reliability and ability to follow through on anything. There was no path for Walter to say to Charley, "Let's give him a job," and have it work that way. But Sharon was tabula rasa, and now they would all make dinner by candlelight. Walter had long wished to be a poor man's Prospero even while observing the world having little use for the type and now he had done nothing and there was a chance and who could say?

As a matter of principle the Raths had no generator and in storms that lasted days it was a joke between them trying to remember what that principle was. But there was charm to the candlelight and flashlights and batteries and beginning to shiver and maybe making love, at least for the first night. It's anyway how Charley remembered those occasions which came often enough on the coast and she described them to Sharon, if leaving the love part a little vague. The worst of the storm was to pass by midnight. Charley rebooked Sharon on a morning flight. Walter made his introductions, Frank, Sharon, Sharon, Frank. They had most of the ingredients for an amatriciana and there were enough little tasks to keep everybody's hands in. Sharon wondered how it happened that she was with members of the family Rath making pasta again, her meal with Stephen still in her mind, and the head of garlic. She was touched, really, yet doubted Charley noticed the light shadow of fate if that's what it was, and Sharon would not mention it. For Frank it was a little like commune days, for an hour or an hour and a half, and he passed a joint around and felt at home, if for a home he could scarcely remember.

The Raths' dinner table was too big for four so they sat in the middle of it like passengers shipwrecked on an island with water all around. The amatriciana came out fairly well and Walter broke out a Barolo and no one said no. They talked about the camp and the woods and Rose Britton and the politics of the day and Walter said nothing like what he'd said to Frank earlier nor did Frank bring any of it up to challenge him or embarrass him. Somehow it came out that Sharon knew Broadway show tunes. She said it came from a time when she was learning to be white, either that or from growing up in New York, but she didn't think many of the Ps in Bronx Cares were up on their Broadway show tunes, so it must have been the first. The Raths had a piano and they wanted her to sing after dinner, or they could all sing, but Sharon looked shy and Charley dropped it. Frank asked about her theatre directing, because it had come out in passing, and Sharon said there was absolutely nothing to it and it was a dead letter as far as she was concerned and she looked embarrassed again, looking into her napkin with her eyes down and a smirky smile, as if remembering a mild unpleasantness. But she did allow that she'd devoted herself to it in prep school and done a couple of shows there, and that's how the surprise of the night came out. She'd gone not only to Mount Holyoke but to Milton Academy, scholarships carrying her from Manhattan Avenue like a string of clouds. Even the Raths hadn't known about Milton, as Sharon had tucked it away. But then Frank said, "My son went to Milton." Frank had a son back in time and a marriage counted more in months than years and the son had grown up in Boston with his mother and the more staid sort of a second dad. "Peter Symonson? He's thirty-four now, so ..." And she did know him. He was three years older and a day student and she didn't know him well but she knew him for sure, he was as tall as Frank and he'd been bony and gangly good-looking and as soon as she heard the name she wondered what he was doing now. "He's married. He's living in the Philippines," Frank said.

"Oh, that's so great, if you talk to him tell him Sharon Mason says hi, would you? He probably won't remember me. I was too young. But we were in *The Skin of Our Teeth* together."

So there was that. It was the most animated she'd been the whole night, which wasn't to say she'd been quiet, which she hadn't been, but only that she remembered Peter Symonson fondly, the way someone fifteen would remember an untouchable upperclassman. They ate strawberries for dessert, the little native ones that had never known a hormone, and sat around. Walter had not found the moment to raise the subject of a job for Frank but he had hopes for the coming days to mature the fruit of the seeds that had been sown. The fog was thick now and dulled the lightning in the windows into a kind of erratic Morse code. Charley said Frank had best stay the night on account of the fog and the deer on the road and all of it. It was her chance to play the mom and they had enough spare rooms and Frank said yes, sure, and thanks, and he'd go out to the Ducati and bring his things in. When he brought them in, they were dripping.

They put Sharon in the ell at one end of the house and Frank at the other. Neither of their rooms was Stephen's room. Charley had yet to show her Stephen's room, and Sharon's impression was that it must be a shrine, or with the furniture covered in sheets or something, where no one entered. Charley had called the power company and the automated message said there would be power by 3 a.m. In her room with her flashlight Sharon couldn't sleep. Everything was small and charming and the furniture was painted so as to induce the sweet sleep of childhood yet still she couldn't sleep and she didn't want to waste the last power in her phone surfing around so she went downstairs looking for a book. Walter's library adjoined the room with the dinner table and she went in and flashed her flashlight along the shelves and found a Strindberg paperback and Walter's Eames chair in a corner. The flashlight was still going strong and she was some pages into *Miss Julie* when the cone of a second flashlight crept past the library door. There was something cartoon-like about it, as if Mr. Magoo were on the prowl. A little zonked, Frank had gotten up to raid the fridge. He was carrying some leftover strawberries in a napkin.

"Oh, hi."

"Hi."

"Couldn't sleep?"

"Nah. Strindberg. Should do the trick."

"Never read him."

"Me neither, tell the truth."

Frank came in and held out the napkin. "Want some?"

"No, thanks. They were good, though."

"Local."

"I guess."

The storm was lessening now. There was only the patter of rain, cat's paws on the windows.

"Please, sit down," she said. "I want to know all about Peter," and it pleased Frank that she spoke to him almost as if to a colleague, without deference to the old guy.

The library had a short couch in the middle that Charley had upholstered in velvet and Frank sat down in it with his flashlight aimed into the rug so that it wouldn't hit Sharon's eyes. She held her place in the Strindberg with a finger and lay her own light in her lap. He told her a few things anyway. Peter was married four years. No children yet. Probably back in the States, probably Houston, in a year or two. Working for an oil company.

She heard Frank's discouragement, or disappointment, in the last. How could his son work for an oil company while the planet's burning up? Frank didn't say it, he didn't need to. It may also have been the case that birth father and son weren't so much in touch these days. There was a sadness to Frank that of course she saw right away, a sadness which Walter could have seen if he'd wanted to but mostly put aside as a given. But the thing about Peter working for the oil company turned their conversation towards the world, and it perked Frank right up. The world as distraction, was it any more than that? He was smart enough to wonder about it himself.

"Tell me about this thing you work for," he said, and Sharon told him about Bronx Cares and the diversionary program and the Ps in the program and a little bit, as well, about the thing that had brought her to Sneeds Harbor, but what she didn't say was that she had been Stephen Rath's lover because whose business was it anyway? By bringing in everything professional and leaving out everything personal she kept the conversation close enough to politics, kind of politics adjacent, and Frank saw the chance to find a friend for intersectionality and the proposition that all the sins of society were related and you couldn't solve one without solving them all.

"I don't know," Sharon said when he was done. "Seems to me if you can solve even one thing, you're doing pretty well."

She had heard about intersectionality, she knew about intersectionality, but she didn't care to get in an argument with him. And besides, she liked his sadness, his seriousness, and the way he could talk for a long time about something in exactly the same tone of voice. Now, towards the end, he was talking about something he had seen on a bus ride in Africa. How he got to it she couldn't quite compute backwards but there it was. Possibly he'd gotten to Obama and how much the world missed Obama despite all his tentativeness and flaws, and speaking of flaws there was Obama's father who was Kenyan and full of flaws, and it was on a bus ride in Kenya down from Lamu to Mombasa that the bus had stopped in seeming nowhere and for no apparent reason because they'd just had a piss stop half an hour before and everyone got off the bus and there across the road, stretching deep into mangrove jungle, were ruins as deep as you could see, of a once-great city, columns and walls and broken pieces, and the mangroves everywhere so that you could walk into it only a little ways, which was probably for the best on account of the very many snakes. As he told her this, she imagined it as the Nazareth in the Maine woods with its bathtubs and sinks and broken everything else. For a few moments in her mind they were exactly the same thing, silent and simply there and promising who could say what, and she liked Frank for making them the same, and then the power came back on.

Lights were on in the next room and somewhere an electric clock was beeping back to life. It was eleven-thirty and she could see for the first time how old Frank was, and he could see how young Sharon was. So there was that, about their little encounter. She laughed just because she did, or for the surprise of the lights, then said she'd go turn off the various lights so they weren't on all night. Frank said he'd help her and he did, then they said good-night and shook hands.

Sharon had her flashlight on again as she made her way back to her room. She was one of those who would rather have a flashlight on in the dark than walk around in the light. It wasn't a question so much of security, it was more about having a companion. There could be all the divides in the world and still something on her side. And what about all these doors? The ell seemed to have too many doors. Surely there was one she oughtn't to open now, the one that even the Raths would not open, nor the cleaning lady, nor a speck of dust. Her only right was her desire. The corridor back to her room seemed long, a ghost's corridor, a door on the left, a door on the right, a second door on the left, as if for a moment the doors wouldn't end until somebody opened them all. She shone her flashlight in the first, a bathroom with an ancient shower; then in a room that might have been a boy's room once but now was only piled high with books, loose books, boxes of books, everything precarious; then, nearly next to hers, as though the Raths had planned it that way, a symmetry of sadness, Stephen's room. Count the ways she knew where she was. She could have turned on a light but for a moment her flashlight was like her heart. His baseball glove, an old laptop, a desk the size for a child, a lamp out of a stick of birch, in the cone of the flashlight like cameos of love. There were no sheets over anything. For that alone she might have said a silent prayer of thanks. Soon she clicked off her light, shut the door, and went to her room to sleep.

On the Bus

Three days later, Frank was offered a job at the Raths' special camp. The only thing they had open was for someone to drive the bus, but Frank said to himself that Ken Kesey drove the bus and some people say "What would Jesus do?" but Frank said to himself "What would Ken Kesey do?" and he took the job, even as he later remembered that it was Neal Cassady who drove the bus and not Kesey himself, which was just as well. It was Sharon's idea to offer the job, she had called up Charley and talked her into it despite Charley's doubts about irresponsibility and vagueness, et cetera.

Overheard

Overheard out at the campsite, where some days it seemed like half the working guys of Sneeds were doing one thing or another.

"Porta potties would've been the economical solution."

"The lady doesn't want porta potties."

"Used to be a flagpole, right over there. When the Whitlocks had it, there was a flagpole."

"Wouldn't be a bad idea, would it now?"

"You've a flagpole, you've something to salute in the morning."

"Absolutely. Best thing you could do for those people."

"Here's the thing. They say they're deprived. Are they the only ones deprived?"

"You referring to yourself, Freddie?"

"I'm referring, for example, to the Somalis."

"The fuck do you care about the Somalis? Since when?"

"It's the roots. That's what's taking all the time, digging out roots. Whereas with the porta potty ..."

"One nation for which it stands."

"That's not right."

"How's it go then?"

"One nation under God indivisible."

"Roots are the natural enemy of the sewer line."

"Here's something else. Why couldn't these people when they arrive, they could clear the woods themselves. Give 'em something to do with themselves all day."

"I don't see all you guys complaining not cashing your checks."

Costs

Walter had his accountant in Ellsworth draw up a budget. There were lines for painting, for roofing, for plumbing, for electric, for structural improvements, for beds, for furniture, for kitchen appliances and dishes, pots and cutlery, for bathroom fixtures, for Wi-Fi, for a first-aid station, for forest clearing, for mowing, for the well, for cleaning up the beach, for the basketball court, for the bus, for plane fares, for Sharon Mason, for six additional salaried personnel, for food and drink, for miscellaneous entertainment, for insurance and the accountant and the lawyer.

The men at work to prepare the place were paid on average twenty-five dollars an hour, though there were contractors such as Donnie's son Kevin, whose crew did the woods, who had the chance to wind up with more.

The overall budget called for $1,123,800 and cost overruns of ten percent or so were to be expected. Walter sold some shares of Apple and that was that. Drop in the bucket.

Moods

As the days of preparation wound down, Charley found herself getting shorter with the men working on the site and complaining about them more to Walter at night. She wanted everything to be right and she believed she wanted that more than the men did. She wasn't sure about Donnie, either. Whose side was he on? She spoke with him less. There were days when she thought she'd do better with a riding crop and leather boots. A lash here, a lash there, that would get them into shape. Though how much did she believe any of it? Anger puddled in her heart. She felt, more and more, as if she might be taking out on the world something that was irreparable. All the mistakes now were her mistakes. She had never run anything before, she felt like a horse running her first race, she was fast and sure but by what right did she expect to win? And was Walter a dear or a rat to put up with her and humor her endlessly saying everything would be alright or with his sweet-and-sour sidewise cackle of a laugh adding "either that or it won't be," when it could never be and she knew it?

In the Bronx there'd been an early streak of the mythic summer-in-the-city days when kids open the hydrants and the tabloids splash the photos of them and the street crime goes up, so that Sharon was busy like crazy, with people taking their vacations and the caseload ballooning, so that she had hardly time to think of Sneeds Harbor except for the once or twice a day when Charley called, always with this or that, mostly inconsequential, driving her a little loony. How was she to know if the kids would want green towels or blue or would there be a gang war on account of it or would white be a prudent solution or a flag of surrender? *Labor omnia vincit.* How groovy that she remembered her ninth-grade Latin, work conquers all, nose to the grindstone, get the crush of new defendants turned into a crush of new participants, more Ds into more Ps, diverted from the pit awhile longer or maybe a few for good, and the night before leaving she would pack her bag. Though she knew it wouldn't work that way. There would be meetings and there would be hand-holding, the rituals of those who'd never gone anywhere. Something odd, though: she somehow found time to think of Frank Symonson, father of the boy she once knew. She thought of him not very often but she did wonder why. As a matter of self-psychoanalysis, she concluded very tentatively it was so that she could stop thinking of Stephen.

After the storm that took out the power, Sneeds Harbor had no rain for two weeks and it had been a dry spring. Calling attention to these facts, Herbert Fallows petitioned the selectmen at their bi-weekly meeting to authorize until further notice Fire Chief Brad Hasselton to require fire permits for any fires that were to be set on private property. Brad Hasselton supported the petition, citing understandings he'd heard that there were persons in town who were going to be having out-of-town guests who were planning to organize bonfires, which given the proximity of the woods and the dryness could create adverse conditions which would at least suggest the prudence of monitoring and permitting. There were sly nods between Brad and Walter acknowledging who was who in this case and who was referred to. The petition—which had been co-signed by eighteen residents, several of whom were in attendance, among them Bob Pearce and Rine Worsley, but not Donnie Cormer, who was present but, citing neutrality, hadn't signed—was accepted unanimously, and the selectmen authorized Brad to issue permits. Walter might have reminded his fellow selectmen and Herbert and Brad of the efforts he and Charley had made over the years and especially given the upcoming camp to keep their woods thinned and clear of dead material, and as well of the showers that were in the forecast for the coming days. But he was someone who believed you couldn't win every battle and would be a fool to try. Brad was a not-unreasonable guy, in Walter's experience, a blowhard at times, as for instance in any bar you might find him in, but he seemed to know what he was doing. Anyway what were the chances you were going to win arguing about fire with the fire chief?

Menus

Charley put together prototype menus but when she looked at them the next morning they looked bizarre and over the top, as if Marie Antoinette had ordered them. Better just to have fun, better just to list a bunch of ingredients that sounded, the way they said it on the Food Channel, yummy.

And what would these be? Squeezed orange juice, native blueberries, native blueberry pancakes, eggs this way and that way but eggs Benedict definitely a possibility, rib-eye steak in the morning or country ham, bacon of course, applewood smoked, espresso, local sourdough plus brioche or croissants or one of those, local crab, local mussels, local brook trout, lobster mac 'n' cheese, lobster stew, lobster period, strawberry shortcake, apple pie baked by local ladies, champagne, rack of lamb, steamers, native corn, baked Maine beans, local greens, local cheeses, more champagne, more lobster, more espresso, and hot-fudge sundaes definitely available all day long, just go to the kitchen and ask for one.

Well, it was a list anyway. A place to start. Don't go crazy, she kept telling herself.

Rules for Activities

To the extent consistent with law-abidingness, etc., no one makes anyone do anything.

No one has to go in the water if they don't want to.

If anybody catches a fish, it's theirs to do what they want to with it.

Kitchen always to be open. Anybody can go in the freezer at any time.

Anyone can take as many siestas as they want and at any time of day.

Great Expectations

It looked like Goshen to Tyrell as he peered out from the back seat of the Suburban at green fields and low green rises and woods, his nose sometimes pressed against the glass and sometimes not. The flight up on a little commuter plane had not been his delight. Only five of them had been on a plane before and of the rest a handful got sick and Tyrell was one of those. He was starting to feel better now, the air outside the airport wasn't like air he knew but he had gulped it in and wondered and got in the Suburban and kept his eyes on the horizon because that's what the driver told him to do. Frank was driving the Suburban. To Tyrell he looked weird enough, with his scruff and his lank, and he was enthusiastic and pointing things out, which seemed a little weird as well because there wasn't much to see, more fields and more trees. Tyrell had spent nine months in Goshen reformatory, while his mama missed him and he missed her, which was more than he could say for the streets of his native borough, which got him to Goshen and now had got him here. The roads were slow and two-lane. They were hardly big enough to call roads. The other boys were kicking each other and talking the usual trash to each other but Tyrell kept his face on the glass and his eyes on the horizon because he was trying to feel better, but also because when you stutter it's easier to think straight than talk straight. They passed a gun shop that said Maine Military. They passed a stale-bread place and parking lots and Tyrell who had stolen one or two and not been caught for it noticed that there weren't many cars, there were more pickup trucks than cars. It was like a movie that way, a buddy movie with a white guy and a Black guy and a truck going a hundred. But the trucks he saw up here were going slow, like they were hunting for something. He thought of the gun shop again. Maine Military, the insinuation of its name. Tyrell was an optimist by nature, willing to give the most unpromising circumstances the benefit of the doubt, but one bottom line in his thinking was that he was against the idea of getting shot at, and for that it didn't matter where he was. An hour later when they pulled into the Raths' camp, Tyrell could see that that too had certain resemblances to Goshen, the chief difference being, in his initial estimate, that Goshen had a lot more of everything. Goshen had every sort of field, baseball, football, an expanse of courts. All Tyrell could see here was one court. Life lessons, as well, told him to look around for guards, but there weren't any. Nor any fences, either. It occurred to him the possibility that there could still be some kind of lasers in the woods that you wouldn't see until you stepped on them.

Rigoberto could not say he was a big fan of lobster the first time he tried to eat one. Frank explained how the locals did it but it seemed like a lot of work and overall more parts of it that you couldn't eat than you could, including the green slime inside that reminded Rigoberto of guacamole that had been sitting in the refrigerator too long. The meat was sweet but it left a sweet stink on your fingers that wouldn't come off even with the handi-wipes, and the plastic bib was simply ridiculous. With a picture of a lobster on it? Rigoberto wasn't sure if it was a party favor or something you were really expected to wear. A rather proud individual in his everyday life, he felt he hadn't come all this way to be humiliated, and the same, really, with the champagne. Rigoberto knew all about champagne, from Bond films he'd seen and similar, but the truth was that he had never tasted it, not the French kind anyway, not the forty-dollar-a-bottle kind. And he would have spit it out when no one was looking, right under the table, but he felt he was too proud and too well brought-up for that. Instead he drank it as if he were lost on a desert island somewhere drinking his own urine to survive. The hot-fudge sundaes were fine, though. To make up for the rest of it, he ate three of those. You could have as many as you wanted. Then Sharon got up for the welcome-wagon part of the evening. Rigoberto may have been bored by then but he was a big fan of Sharon. Having a decent appreciation of his own talents, he felt a reciprocal appreciation of her for seeming to have recognized them. As well, around juvenile detention she had the reputation more or less of an angel, insofar as you might be almost on the bus to Rikers or upstate and she could walk into the courtroom and talk to the judge and DA and ten minutes later you'd be walking on the street. These were no mean considerations, and so he tried to listen to what she was saying, which had to do with the great privilege these people up here had for hosting all of them and so they could forget about everything else and the past and home and everything because for two weeks they were the kings and princes and what not, and if the staff could do anything to help or they needed anything, only just ask. All of this information made a rather startling impression on Rigoberto's mind, especially the part if he heard it right about it being the Anglos' privilege and not his for him to be there, but right in the middle of all that Sharon was saying about the staff helping and only having to ask, Rigoberto received a text from his little sister back home with the emoji of a cat's wide smile, and what Liddie messaged was "just be careful up there," to which she'd linked a story from not too far in the past, about the governor of the exact state where Rigoberto happened to find himself and what this governor was saying was that the drug dealers were coming up to his state from Connecticut and New York with names like D-Money and Smoothie and Shifty, those type of guys, the governor said, his precise words, they come up, they sell their heroin, they go back home and half the time they impregnate a young white girl before they leave, which was a real sad thing because then there'd be another issue they'd have to deal with down the road. So in Rigoberto's mind this rather contradicted the welcome-wagon theory of everything. When it came to the question-and-answer time, he asked Sharon about what the governor had said, which he read out loud so that everybody could hear. No shortage of obscenities rained down on the governor then, though the champagne dampened some reactions into mocking and sarcastic laughs that hollowed out the room. No one seemed more pissed and upset than Sharon, who gritted her teeth and acted like she hadn't had this information before and for a moment Rigoberto was even afraid she was pissed at him for bringing it up and spoiling the party. But it wasn't that. It was only her surprise, which was almost more an awakening than really a surprise. She said she would look into it. And then Rigoberto was pleased with himself for bringing it to her attention.

On the second day they all went for a hike in the morning and a sail on the Raths' Concordia in the afternoon and to a steel-drum concert in the evening down by the village dock and what Markus thought of it all was that it was slow. As he ruminated on the very word "slow," it seemed to him as if he had discovered the biggest secret of white people, it wasn't only that they ran slow, slow was just the way they were, it was like an overall condition, they seemed to *like* slow, they woke up in the morning slow. Or, to let his mind wander a bit in a direction that was hardly a pretty picture, they probably fucked slow too. Everybody said Markus was slow, like steal-the-robot-thinking-it's-an-air-conditioner slow, a slowness of perception, anyway, that to some degree he had incorporated into his self-image, but now he could just see the white person in him, he imagined there must have been some white person centuries back there, having his time with his great-great-great-great-somebody or other, and two hundred years later here was Markus Twomley and everybody wondered what was wrong with him. Go slow, they say. Markus asked himself who was always saying that and the answer was clear: white people. He considered the sail on the Raths' Concordia the most obvious example. How long were they on that boat? About two or three hours but it felt like two or three months, and to get how far, five miles maybe? Even if you had one leg, you could run five miles faster than that boat. The big diaper of a sail particularly galled him. *Turn on the motor, you dumb fucks! You dumb, slow fucks! You trying to save on the gas? The fuck is wrong with you? We could be home by now.* Markus considered also what they'd done in the morning, walking up some hill. What was the point? It was probably less exercise than taking a shit. Though maybe that was it, maybe that was the white-man's trick, Markus thought, to slow everything down till it was the easiest thing in the world, you take your time and you take over everything, you've got time left over to boss everybody around. And what did they have for them when the sun went down and it was the darkest location he had ever been in in his nineteen years of life? A bunch of old white folks thinking they were Black, having their good times, playing the pans, didn't they know that was Black man's music? Though of course it wasn't really Black man's music, because it was so slow. Markus had a bet with himself that not one of them had ever been a thousand miles close to Trinidad. Nor did it surprise him what happened next. Markus felt, actually, a bit like a sage, a community wise man, alleged slowness and all, when it

91

happened. Or like a traveler in a land strange but too familiar at the same time.

What happened was this, according to the reconstruction of Luis Espinoza when later, back at the Raths' camp, he was cozily embedded in the hand-sewn Italian linen sheets that Charley had special ordered from a place in Boston. Luis first specified to himself, a kind of stipulation like you might make in the court-house or equivalent, that he wasn't the one who started it with the ice cream, not exactly, but yes, of course, he would have to admit he was there and participated. And in terms of what then went down, in his impartial opinion, some of the others were already feeling distressed on account of various situations, for instance the music from the locals, where they all had to sit there and listen to it and what else could they do? Or for another, the situation where during the music if you looked around for half a second you could see that a bunch of the seats right around where they were sitting were empty whereas in the whole rest of the parking lot just about every other seat was taken, so that you could draw your own conclusions. So then after what only a person who'd never heard music in their last thousand lifetimes could call a concert, a number of the boys including himself were eating their ice cream on the street and the other folks from the town were leaving the concert and none of the boys paid them any mind, didn't harass them in any way, shape, or manner, it was all peaceful, until a boy from the Edenwald projects named Jayden spilled his cone on the sidewalk. This was one hundred percent an accident, as far as Luis could see, so of course Jayden left it there, what was he supposed to do, it was the sidewalk, it wasn't his grandma's house. But then—and here, even tucked in comfortably hours later, Luis couldn't help but feel annoyed all over again, so that he began replaying her exact words in his head—some old witch came by, like she was the state police, and said why did he put it on the sidewalk, and why didn't he put it in the trash, and there was the trash right over there. And she pointed to some trash can somewhere that Luis himself couldn't even see. And then she looked at Jayden and all of them and got out a tissue that looked crinkly like it had already been used, like possibly she blew her nose on it first, and picked up the lump of ice cream from the sidewalk like it was dogshit and found the can that was across the street somewhere. So Jayden said, "Thank you, ma'am," sarcastic-like, even though the ice cream by the time she picked it all up was melting down to just about soup, so that the way she was picking it up was making it even more of a mess than it already was.

Now Luis Espinoza was generally a live-and-let-live type of person, a little like a gliding bird, he didn't go looking for disputes and when they came his way he'd flown from more than a few, but in this instance he thought to himself this wasn't right, Jayden didn't do anything wrong, so even though Jayden was one of the Black dudes and someone he'd never met in his life before the airplane, Luis himself felt righteous, or possibly also a little comradely, insofar as Jayden, despite being a total stranger to him, was together with him in this strange town far from home. And as well there was something in Jayden's sarcastic tone when he said, "Thank you, ma'am," that Luis liked, maybe the way the words came out of Jayden's mouth, kind of curled up like a snake. All of it gave Luis a bit of courage, or maybe also a desire to be seen, by Jayden but possibly by all the others as well.

And so he took his cone like it was a Marlboro cigarette and butted it out on the nearest store window. Now everyone was laughing at the way the ice cream ran down the window, and some of the others then threw their cones when they were almost done with them, and dropped their napkins in the street. That's all it was, really. There was a lot of laughing after that, having a good time, enjoying the evening, free at last from the terrible concert. And then Frank came along and said it was time to go. But first he saw what had gone on and got out a towel and started cleaning up the window and the ice cream and whatever was on the street, and Luis, because he felt like he had started it even if he didn't, and then the other boys too, started helping Frank to clean up. Because they could see what he was doing and Frank was not a bad dude so they wanted to help him, they didn't want to just stand around while he was doing all the work.

In all of this Luis felt that he saw a kind of silver lining, since it was the first time all the boys laughed together, it didn't matter which projects or streets they came from. And he himself had stuck up for a stranger, a small story he might one day remember about himself, a stranger whose sarcastic tone he'd liked. Luis soon entered into a peaceful sleep, in the coolest sheets he'd ever slept in in his life.

Microaggressions

Charley never went to the selectmen's meetings because they were tedious and long and she didn't wish to be disappointed in the town she tried so hard to love, but she went to this one. This time it was Herbert Fallows again who had marshaled his troops and got more signatures on a petition and would be urging the selectmen to exercise their power of the purse and dip into the town's discretionary fund for the purpose of contracting regular sheriff's patrols for the coming two weeks, on a day-and-night basis. Normally the sheriff only sent a car through Sneeds a couple of times a week. There wasn't crime enough to justify more, though if something did occur, a boathouse broken into or a car hitting a deer, a deputy would come around to take reports. But now the incident downtown with the ice cream had caused a stir with portions of the citizenry. Charley sat towards the back so that she would be out of eye contact with her husband. No chance for a conspiratorial glance, nothing to suggest the fix was in.

It was a good-sized crowd and rather evenly divided, the old Sneeds Harbor way, hair parted down the middle, and it pleased Walter to see. It seemed word had spread of Herbert's petition and there were enough of those dismayed by it, or by Herbert himself, who presented himself so often as the people's tribune when there were obviously people around who weren't *his* people, to make a tidy opposition. There were the predictable lefties, Pat Morris and Harry Casey, both of whom voiced variations on the theme that no harm had been done nor crime committed, so what were people exercised about? But there were also new converts like Mitchell Bassett, an unlikely ally in that he was one of the lobstermen and the lobstermen usually hung together in suspicion of outsiders of any sort. Mitchell felt hiring the sheriff for all those hours might be a budget-buster and moreover set a bad precedent for future raids on the town treasury, like you wouldn't want to start budgeting extra for the sheriff every time someone whiffed marijuana on the Clarkswood Road when you already had the feds' helicopters whirring overhead. You could classify Mitch's conversion, in particular as he referenced the choppers, more on economic or even economic self-interest grounds, in that he had property on the Clarkswood Road and was rumored to cultivate the blessed weed in isolated patches there. But then there was Doris Bunting, who had been opposed to the Raths' camp for reasons of geography but now saw something noble and in the fine Sneeds tradition of open-handedness and generosity of spirit in what the Raths had accomplished, and at no cost to the town. Moreover—and here possibly was hidden the proximate reason for her conversion—Doris had long felt that the individual who "started it" with the kids and the ice cream, Bea Thorne, was a bit of a nut and a busybody, though she didn't phrase it quite that way at the meeting. "Consider the messenger," was as close as she came, then couldn't help herself and added, "It's always the people looking for trouble who find it." Kerry Micheau added that this was all about microaggressions and there seemed to be a lot of microaggressors around. This provoked a few grumphs and suppressed chuckles, in that Kerry was generally believed, even by those who loved her and swore by her, to have at best a limited understanding of things she read online, which usually didn't stop her from talking about them at the first opportunity.

The petition's opponents mostly spoke first, which left Herbert Fallows time to regroup his arguments so that their opposition could be taken in account. His main point unsurprisingly was better safe than sorry, but appended to that was the modest cost of two weeks of extra sheriff's protection; and—as if to prove there was no bad faith going on—Sneeds' proud history of civil rights' engagement, exemplified by the five Sneeds residents who took a bus to Alabama in 1962 and were arrested there in a protest, and a number of others he could name but chose not to at the moment, for brevity's sake; and the fact that defacing a store window is vandalism, and vandalism is indeed a crime, so that the assertion of no crime committed was incorrect. "Now admittedly it was a misdemeanor, it was not a quote unquote *big* crime," Herbert continued, "and no one's trying to make a mountain out of an anthill here, we're not asking for the kid's scalp, we're just being prudent, out of an abundance of caution. You know in New York, where these kids come from, you know what cleaned up that city was the 'broken-window' policing. When crime was rampant, they let the small things go by. By cracking down on the broken windows, et cetera, crime overall went into a decline which criminologists say was historic." That was typical of Herbert, to bring in things like "historic" and "criminologists" to firm up his argument. And people admired that about him. Herbert did his homework. He finished by referencing the Black people who'd been employed at the Nazareth Hotel a hundred years previous, and who'd had no difficulties living in Sneeds at the time. It was an old story, of course, but one that ought not to be forgotten.

It was time then for the selectmen to ask any questions if they had them, and then to vote. Selectman Cummings right off asked Herbert if he was pointing to the Nazareth Hotel as an example of racial tolerance or otherwise or what was his point there exactly? Herbert said you had to remember that the country as a whole was more prejudiced then, but that compared to the country, from what we know, Sneeds was fairly advanced. Selectman Roberts asked about the broken-window theory of policing, which he hadn't previously heard of. Herbert said crime plummeted after that was instituted, one theory being that greater respect for the law in general was cultivated, though of course there were those who would suggest other theories, demographics and incarceration rates and the like.

Both Selectman Cummings and Selectman Roberts expressed the view that policing in New York City and policing in Sneeds Harbor were different matters entirely, though Selectman Roberts was willing to concede its general relevance. Selectman Roberts then noticed that, somewhat belatedly, Bea Thorne had entered the hearing room, and seated herself way to the back, two rows behind Charley. She had her arms folded and a set expression, as if you wouldn't get a word out of her if you levered open her mouth with a crowbar. Nonetheless, Roberts asked, "How you doing, Bea? All this fuss, huh?"

Bea was something of a fixture around Sneeds, living alone and old, sitting often on the benches when the weather allowed. She squinted when addressed, then surprised the room by speaking in a loud voice, as if her hearing aid was off, "This was always a clean village!"

"Thank you, Bea," Roberts said, thinking it was a mistake to have asked her anything, then called for the vote.

Selectman Cummings said, "I'm afraid I'm one of those 'if it ain't broke don't fix it' people. The deputies always come if we need 'em, if something happens. So why spend the extra money?"

Julie Hastings, the recorder, asked, "So that's a no?"

"That is a no," Cummings affirmed.

Selectman Roberts said, "I'd say it's a close call, and we've got to do a balance here between fairness to all concerned on the one hand and the safety of all concerned on the other. I guess I come down on, like the man said, better safe than sorry. Vote yes."

So it was left to Selectman Rath. He said only, "Don't see the harm." He said it in his low, sad voice and voted yes.

Charley, in the back, thought at first she must have misheard him.

They walked back to the house in silence, two birds that had lost the song that let the other know they were alive. She wondered if he was clueless, if her silence had lost the power to tip him off. Her mind was so stuffed with things to say that she couldn't imagine one that would be the one, and to do what exactly, state her case or her loss or let go a rage that would purify and dissolve and find a way through? The word "betrayal" presented itself as a handy choice, and she hated it for that and knew that it would be inadequate. So they walked and Walter wondered what she thought and had a pretty good idea which he let pass for a lack of confirmation because who could ever know the other and least of all the other who was close to touch, and he felt the joy of a careless limbo, of a waiting game. Of course she would want to know why. But it was a trap to say, because it was impossible for him to say or even know, he could only guess, and Charley hated guesses.

They went inside the white clapboard house and she went upstairs and he went to the ell, and they prepared for bed in their respective bathrooms and then they met up again.

"Bastard," she said, and it was inadequate. This was before they shut off their respective lights and the bed felt very wide, as wide as the sea or one of those that people talk about, that are also inadequate, and lazy, and lost.

"No harm done," he said, and it was inadequate.

"Coward," she said, and it was inadequate.

"Jew bastard," he said, and it was inadequate.

"Don't use that pathetic excuse with me," she said, and it was inadequate too, though less so than the others.

"I thought, having a deputy around isn't a big deal and it'll quiet the naysayers down and give them something for their ice cream cone. The kids won't notice, and after a day nobody else will care. All politics are local, my love," he said, and whether it was or not, it felt inadequate and lazy and lost, as he had known that it would. And they shut off their respective lights.

In the dark he added, "Better take the champagne off the menus. Just to be on the safe side."

By this he meant from the menus alone, not from the meals themselves. The next day he would tell Frank to be alert if a sheriff's car came around, and to be sure to hide any alcohol if it did.

Donnie Cormer was back at the Canterbury but this time he was drinking alone. He'd skipped the selectmen's meeting as he didn't want that feeling anymore of being neutral. He'd read too much online. He could see too clearly now Rine Worsley's point of view. He didn't want to be conflicted, and drinking was the obvious choice to help it happen. Yes, it was true the Raths had been good to him. Yes, it was true he'd worked for them more than twenty years and as the result of it no longer lived in a Fleetwood Festival down the trailer park road but rather in a tract house very nearly on the outskirts of the village and his truck was but two years old. He'd totted all that up. He could not deny he'd incurred debts to the Raths, not monetary but more serious. But hadn't he paid them back? Like the most faithful dog you could find, like a black lab, one of those, always by their side, negotiating this or that, putting in words here there and everywhere, taking Mr. Rath hunting or even teaching their kid how to clean a gun. He could go on and on. It had been awhile, after all. It had been a chunk, and you don't have that many in a life. Now he remembered the year the power was out for ten days and he put the Mister and Missus up in the trailer, when they still had the trailer, and Caryn had made them her blueberry crumble for breakfast, which they agreed was the best breakfast they'd ever had.

But that was then and now was whatever it was. These kids. It was a provocation. That was the word for it, a word he'd not previously known, but Donnie had been educating himself. Old Rine, love him or hate him, but he kept his head above the waves. It had come to the point where Donnie didn't even like to go out to the camp. He didn't like what he saw, the basketball where the tennis court had been, and the kids out there playing, which if they want to play, fine, okay, only they didn't fit the picture of the camp and the water and the woods and, frankly, of everything he knew. Let them play basketball back wherever. He'd seen those movies, the white man can't jump, whatever that was, he liked that one, he had nothing against anybody as long as they didn't screw up. But there was something screwed up here. And he knew all about the boy, and he loved the boy, his own boy's friend, but you can't use the same excuse forever when there are others in the world, too, to consider. It would be a financial hit, that was for sure. It was for this reason that Donnie hadn't told Caryn. It was also for this reason that he felt, if vaguely, heroic. Taking one for the team and all of that.

Donnie downed another shot of Jim Beam and considered whether he should go home and compose a note. A note would be as final as it could be, there would be no talking him out of it once a note was given and passed, with the keys in the envelope and all of it. But a note didn't comport with the hero he felt he might be. A man told another man important things in person. A man looked the other in the eye and didn't flinch and all that crap which he felt so full of at the moment that he might shit all over the Canterbury bar if he didn't go at once and do the deed. So he left too much money on the bar and got in his truck and drove to the village where the lights were all out in the Raths' old white colonial that Donnie had taken such care of that the two hundred years it had sat there seemed more like the two decades he'd done the job. That's what people would say, it was like a new house, condition-wise, which wasn't so easy to achieve. As he got out of his truck, it was as if he were admiring it for the last time. There was a good bath of moonlight that night and there was also the streetlamp up the block that would stay on till midnight, and the Raths' house, that Donnie had long taken in some secret sense to be *his* house, or anyway one of *his*, for the care he took, looked milky and pure and almost as if he had never seen it before.

He rapped the brass knocker several times, and louder the longer he waited. He knew full well Mr. Rath liked to stay up reading, and there could have been lights on in the ell that weren't visible from the street, and it was only eleven o'clock, and there were other excuses in his mind for knocking so loud and long but mostly he did it for the urgency on his tongue. If not now, when?

Presently the front hall was lit and Walter, hurriedly into his robe, opened the door to Donnie. His immediate reaction, shaped by events of the evening and the day past, was that some new catastrophe had befallen the camp. Then he smelled the bourbon on Donnie, which wasn't unfamiliar but had never, in Walter's observation, stopped him from doing his job. "Hey, Don, what's going on?" he asked, his voice husky from the night.

"Mr. Rath, sir, could we talk, sir?" Donnie said.

"Sure. What's going on?" Walter asked again, and opened the door wider for Donnie to enter. Donnie hadn't called him "sir" in twenty years.

Donnie came as far as the front hall, where he stood with his hat still on his head. Charley had also been awakened and she stood for a few seconds at the top of the stairs, silent, unwilling to give Walter the satisfaction of asking what was going on. It was enough for her to see that it was Donnie, and as soon as she heard him say, "No, sir, it's not to do with any camp business, not directly," she disappeared.

Walter waited for Donnie to say what it was, if it wasn't the camp and it was eleven at night.

"Sorry to awaken you, sir, but I'm done."

"You're *done*?" Walter asked.

Donnie was taller than Walter and bigger and there were times that he seemed to tower over him as if he were a genie out of a bottle, and this was one of those.

"Yes, sir, I'm grateful for the long employment, but I cannot continue." And he fished some keys from his jeans and held them out.

Walter looked at them before taking them.

"Twenty-four years, Donnie. That's a lot of time. It's late, you sure you don't want to ..."

Donnie spoke over him as the word "reconsider" left Walter's teeth. "No, sir, I'm quite firm."

"What's with the 'sir' shit, Donnie? Where'd that come from?"

But Donnie wasn't bending. He'd rehearsed it all and he wasn't going to be sweet-talked by old allegiances or whatever. He knew Mr. Rath could very nearly talk the pants off a person, he'd seen it more than once. He said nothing and stood there and tried not to fidget. The keys were still in his hand.

It felt stupid not to, so Walter finally took them.

"With great reluctance," he said.

"Appreciate that, sir," Donnie said stiffly.

"You know, Donnie, we really depend on you, and you've been great, you know how much we appreciate you," Walter said. "Almost family, right?" But it wouldn't budge the taller man.

"No question," Donnie said.

"Then could I ask why?" Walter said, which he hadn't wanted

to say but it was all he was left with. He didn't want Donnie to leave. It felt like a defeat and he was tired of counting his defeats.

"Just seems time," Donnie said.

"That's all? It's eleven at night, and you've been out drinking for sure, and suddenly it's time?"

"Could be a matter of principle, as well."

"Ah."

But Donnie only stood there then. When Walter asked what principle that was, or what principles those were, he responded only by taking off his hat, as if it were something he'd forgotten.

"I'll send a check, then," Walter said. "Or you want to stop by for it?"

"Either way," Donnie said.

Walter then extended a hand which Donnie reluctantly took. The handshake felt cursory and cold and as if Donnie hadn't meant it that way but it was still the way it had to be.

"Okay, then," Walter said. "If you change your mind, you call me tomorrow? Or whenever."

"Yes, sir. I will do that, if there's a change."

"And you couldn't stay on two weeks, through the camp?" Walter asked, thinking it would give Donnie the time to retreat.

"You'll do alright, no question," Donnie said, and put his hand on the doorknob that he'd fixed and plated and polished many times.

"Good-night, Donnie," Walter said.

"Could I ask you one thing, Mr. Rath?" Donnie said when he was outside the door and was lit by the moon and the streetlamp again.

"Anything at all," Walter said.

"Are Jews white people?" Donnie asked.

The touching part was that it was Walter that Donnie asked and he wasn't being sarcastic, either. It was like he really wanted to know and Walter might be a source of wisdom on the subject, as he'd been a source of wisdom about the world beyond Sneeds Harbor for years. Or, at worst, and possibly, Donnie was giving the defendant a chance to defend himself, as a matter of elemental fairness, or perhaps a charitable exemption to an old friend. Walter couldn't get the question out of his head. *Are Jews white people?* It had so seldom come up in his life that he'd almost forgotten it could be a question at all. The moonlight no longer streaked the curtains. A cloud had rendered the familiar room he was in, lying on his back as if paralyzed, as if a move in either direction might kill him, a shade of black that was without shadows. Charley was snoring lightly. It seemed like a benediction that she was.

He had answered, "As far as I know they are," and they had both left it at that and then Donnie left. Had Walter lost the chance he had to rescue Donnie from some dark corner of the digitals, some 4chan or 8chan special? He'd said what he could, as far as he knew, but why didn't he know more? The world felt hollow beneath him. The mattress on his side of the bed could fall away into a cavity and he could be swallowed up by his own easy assumptions. In the dark he couldn't even see the color of his skin to make sure that it was whatever it was, whatever it had always been. Walter could remember, in the abstract—the way so much of his life was in the abstract—asking himself Donnie's question, but nobody had ever put it to him in the world. *As far as he knew, as far as he knew.* They came from the Middle East, didn't they? They call them Semites, don't they? And who you calling a Semite, paleface? Paleface, the joke's on you.

Walter imagined googling the question whether Jews are white people. Good for a chuckle, that one. And what would Google say? Would it say that Jews are white because when they came to

Europe gentiles raped them, or they had secret affairs, or inter-married more than you might think, or it was a matter of natural selection, the paler Jews preferred in mating because they were more adapted to their new surroundings, or were there streams of converts, or were they always white enough, even in the old homeland, dark-eyed maybe but white? Ethiopian Jews were dark-skinned. Walter took comfort in that. Did it not prove it wasn't a matter of race? Some Jews were, some Jews weren't. Simple as that and go to sleep. Race as a construct, race as a dream, race as the oppressor's tool. But he couldn't sleep. Donnie leaving, Charley pissed off, the detritus of the day. Was the ongoingness of life a comfort or a curse? Don't like the weather? Wait a few minutes. But he waited and nothing changed. He considered Donnie, good old Donnie who was always there and stalwart and kept his resentments in, a victim of the very thing that had made Walter's fortune. Small comfort in that. The internet as destroyer of souls.

Charley rolled over in her sleep and ceased to snore. They wouldn't be coming after blue-eyed Charley. Or what if they did, blaming her for him, as if he'd sullied her with his skin. It was all going nowhere. The monstrosity of it. He wished she would forgive him, but didn't dare ask. It would be too cruel. Let him figure this one out himself.

And the kids out at the camp, who could have been left well enough alone, summer in the city, and who would have been the wiser? They should, they shouldn't have, they should, they shouldn't have, the "they" being Walter and Charley, the whole world fifty-fifty. Why couldn't people see both sides? The Jew, white or not white. Give both sides fifteen minutes to make their case. Karl Marx was a white man, wasn't he? Married into the aristocracy, talked a good game, anyway. And you know the funny thing about him? No, the wonderful thing about him, the way Walter read him anyway: he had a sympathy for rich as well as poor. He saw the misery of the rich, how they could never get enough, how in the capitalist game it was always kill or be killed and if you played it no matter how well you were left a jungle animal, wary and afraid of tomorrow. Old Karl, the old white Jew, would relieve the misery of all, or anyway saw how the world would get it done. What an optimist, what a humanitarian, loving everybody to death. Walter tried then to persuade himself that it would be better not to be white at all. To fight the good fight, for the masses of the world, the future there for the taking. A passing thought, even a lovely thought, but it didn't put him to sleep.

Meanwhile back at the ranch, where the home team played ball. Were there enough Donnies out there to overthrow the whole country? Probably not, but who could say? It made Walter patriotic in a way, defiant and defensive, a minuteman of the mind, even to think of it. The welcoming, beautiful country. But what had become of it or was it becoming? Walter knew he sounded like a leftie until he didn't. What was he then? The devoted secret follower of the likes of Herbert Fallows? Hardly. He was a nobody. He stood for nothing. And he couldn't help it. What he couldn't help was to see. A thousand examples, a thousand hard thoughts, the thoughts of a man near to turning old. These kids at the camp, bless them. Could you get in trouble with the censors of the mind for thinking these were humanity's youth and hope? Why couldn't people see both sides? The Jew, white or not white?

What would Walter Rath do if he were king? Well, maybe he'd have kings, to start with. Somebody to blame it all on. A bad king, bad times, but at least it was something you could get past, something that left a future, there could always be a good king next. There was hope, and how silly and simple-minded was that? Walter Rath, the royalist of Sneeds Harbor. The Jew-royalist, that too, of course, if you were going to write the Wikipedia article the way it should be written. David, Solomon, Walter Rath, continuity.

Or should he think not of kings alone but of philosopher-kings? Wasn't that closer, wasn't that almost it? Not David, Solomon, Walter but Socrates, Plato, Walter. How undemocratic, all the modern complaints. The Athenian democracy, built on slaves. The world was not what it seemed and never had been. And was he queer? Pretty late to be noticing it, but what if? Loving the Greeks, wasn't that a sign? Those young, masculine Greeks, the flower of the youthful world—and that little habit of theirs that they found beautiful and we find nasty. Skip to Augustine, get out of town. Walter loved Augustine almost before all others. The purity of his conversion, as if he would take whatever the universe gave him without complaint. And wasn't it the case of Christianity that it dug deeper into the human condition than the Greeks, it dealt with suffering and death and not in a childish way. But could he ever believe all of it? The One Redeemer, and only through faith in Him. But if the world was as bent as the physicists say and time is not the time that we knew, couldn't our language itself bend, so that "One" didn't quite mean "One" and you could have faith in Him and also faith in All? Fat chance you'd get past the priests with that one. The universe bent but the language buckled under the weight of all his hopes. And Charley didn't believe any of it, and if she did, would she have taken him on?

Or was exactly the opposite possible, the way opposites were always possible in his mind: was it only because she secretly believed that she found something good in him? *Are Jews white people?* He loved Donnie just then, for the purity of the question. And one new thought that stirred the darkness: it wasn't that the neos and Nazis hated the Jews alone. They hated the Jews for giving them the Christians. It was the Christians and all that universal love they truly hated, but there was no way they could take on the Christians, at least not right away, so they took on the next best thing.

And who cares what Walter Rath thinks anyway? He'll die in his bed thinking his thoughts and no one will know. And what are his thoughts good for anyway, except to distract him from what he feels? Fear, and whatever fear begets, but first the fear. The cowardly Walter, just like the lady said, cowering, waiting to be hit, ducking down. He must be better than that, but how? At last he felt he might sleep.

Is Walter a secret Christian? Does he secretly believe more than the believers? Who's he kidding, he's chased women, and money, and a half-pint of fame, he's believed in the world, and has he ever truly repented? He doesn't know how to repent. It's Charley, over there, in the wide bed, lightly snoring again, who has set out to repair the world, the ancient mission of the Jews. It was as if they had switched places. Augustine, dear Augustine, teach me how to repent. His last thought before sleep.

A Note from the Town's Tree Committee

Charley received it in the next morning's mail. It began by thanking her for her years of service. It went on to say that the Committee understood the demands on her time made by the new project she'd undertaken and so felt at the present time, with important matters upcoming on its own agenda, it would serve everybody's interests if Sarah Underwood took her place on the committee. It closed by thanking her again for her years of service. It was signed simply THE COMMITTEE.

A Gift

Sharon had a gift for tears. This was as a therapist once suggested she view her emotionality. When things went badly or well, whether the world's purpose was clear or obscure, or her purpose was clear or obscure, or if there was purpose to any of it or so much purpose to everything that it overwhelmed her and all she could do was lie in her pool of misery looking up or down, in all of it she must remember her gift for tears. The old Noël Coward song about the movie star who was terribly lonely, she'd sung that one too, she knew all the tunes and there were days when they all made her cry.

"Sharon?" That was Frank Symonson coming in when he had no business coming in. It was Frank's way, having lived so long alone. He had shed certain social graces. He sometimes forgot to knock on doors.

She was in the old camp cabin reserved for management, and she alone was the management. It was the evening past when the selectmen voted for the sheriff's patrols and during the day the Ps had been over in Hancock learning to play golf and the deputies had begun passing by Sneeds, even once stopping at the camp, young and polite and unobtrusive, "just seeing if anybody needed anything," no cases of bubbly anywhere to be seen, and now the boys were home from golf and having lobster and clams and oysters and champagne for dinner again and what seemed to get Sharon going this time was the possibly apocryphal story somebody told her about the inmates of the Maine State Prison a hundred fifty years ago who rioted because all they were ever

given for dinner was lobster. A story of the relativity and tentativeness of life as well as of when lobsters were so plentiful they
were thought to be a poor-man's food and no match for the noble
salmon, all of which might have been good for a laugh but it
started her bawling helplessly, her face flat on her desk, and that
was how and where Frank found her.

She straightened up, embarrassed and surprised, though
perhaps not as embarrassed and surprised as she would have been
if it was the first time. In the Bronx she was known to gush on
occasion and for reasons sometimes hard to discern. Stephen had
loved that about her. Frank said sorry and went to leave, a kind
of hat-in-hand gesture, but by the time he reached the door, she
was composed.

"If you want to know, in more general terms," she said, "it was
on account of this whole fucking wipeout of a project."

"Is why you were crying?" he asked, because his years of living
alone had also nurtured in him a degree of directness, occasionally
bordering on cluelessness, as if from long disuse he had forgotten
certain dance steps.

"Who are you, Shifty or Smoothie or D-Money?" she said.
"Just get off the interstate? Got a little smack for sale?"

"Oh no. That shit? That idiot? The governor's an idiot!"

"Can you imagine, if you were one of these kids, what that
sounded like? They didn't have to come up here. I dragged them
up here! I made it sound good! You know who it's good for? *Us*,
not them! And it's not only they get insulted, get policed, everybody's suspicious, nobody'll go near them except to complain
about an ice cream cone, but they're bored! They're bored out of
their skulls! You see them making the best of it, and I love them
for that, I totally love them, nobody's complaining, they're there
at that stupid pans concert I never should have approved, they're
playing golf or kayaking or whatever else it is or trying to, they're

out there running up and down the court every spare minute, just pretending it's home. Treat them like little princes? Sure, why not, good idea. We forgot to think: little princes get bored! Chocolate again for dinner, honey? Caviar for dessert? Give me a burger, for fuck's sake! You know the one thing they're going to learn from all this? The rich don't have it that much better than they do. Only difference is, they don't get thrown in jail or shot."

Frank had smoked a little after dinner and it left his smile a little goofy.

"What are you grinning at, jackass?"

"Your vast articulation of grievance."

"Thank you very much."

Then to cheer her or only to change the subject or because it was the reason he'd come over in the first place and to justify having found her in tears, he said, "I spoke to Peter. He says hi."

There was just a moment when she was careful. "Peter your son?"

"He says hi."

"Say hi back, would you?"

"Sure. Will do."

"Oh, I'm glad. How is he?"

"Fine. His wife's expecting."

"No shit. Frank, that's great."

"It is great."

"Boy? Girl? When?"

"No idea. I don't know. I didn't ask."

"Men never ask anything," she said.

"They do," he said.

"Not really," she said.

"I'll give you a for instance," he said. "Peter asked me to ask you if you were doing any theatre directing. He said you were the real deal."

"He didn't say that," she said. "The real deal?"

"He did. Exactly."

"People don't say that."

"Okay. Really talented."

"I knew he didn't say that."

"But are you? Doing any?"

"Didn't you ask me that once before?"

"I told him, maybe when you got back to the city."

"Tell him no, not at the present moment."

"When you get back to the city?"

"No. I don't think."

"I bet you'd be good."

"I don't think."

"Pete's not an easy critic."

But Sharon finally refused to go there. She was being distracted from her grievance and the alternative would have been inexcusable. She could feel her gift, she could feel it soon to be given. Instead, "What am I going to do? What are we going to do with these kids? We've got ten more days! What are we going to do for ten fucking days?"

"Teach them to be WASPs?" he said.

"They've already learned!" she shouted, loud enough to be heard in the fields if anyone had been passing by.

It may have been lucky, then, that Frank was twenty percent or thirty percent whacked, because he had one of those ideas that pushed along all the other ideas that sounded whacked enough on their own like playing golf and eating caviar and sailing and dropping ice cream on the sidewalk. There was even a moment when he dared to think it was a pretty good whacked idea, worth daring her to yell at him even louder.

"Put on a play," he said.

"What?"

"A play," he said.

"What kind of play?"

"You know, like a play."

"A play?"

"You could do it."

It was the getting personal part that finally infuriated her, what she could or couldn't do, the real deal or not quite the real deal. "*I* could do it? What about *them*! They didn't come up here for theatre camp! They don't go to *Lear* in Central Park for a night of good fun!"

"So don't do *Lear*," Frank said.

"What are we supposed to do, then? Shifty and Smoothie and D-Money come to town?"

"Yes," Frank said, because "yes" was the shortest word he could think of and for a second it didn't sound that insane, which could have been attributable to his condition but so what, and when he could see she was again near tears he took a few steps towards her and reached out and held her, for only so long, like a breath or two, his two fat hands on her two slender arms, as if he had just given her a pep talk and was sending her out to play the fateful last minutes of the game.

She shook herself away, thinking of Shifty and Smoothie and what a bad idea it was. If she'd only known, she might have compared what she felt then to what Walter Rath felt when he heard Stephen's idea for the camp.

The next morning when she proposed it to Walter and Charley, Walter got a laugh from it, and it didn't seem to be an entirely cynical laugh. It gave her a teaspoon of courage. Charley wanted to know, if there was going to be a play, wouldn't someone have to write a play? Sharon said they could improvise, and she would write a few lines at night or try, and it wouldn't have to be a long play, and it was possible it was the worst idea ever, but she was desperate. Walter asked if the kids would go along with it. She said she had no idea but she would find out. Charley said she thought they could get the little stage at the back of the school that was used for the assemblies and the Christmas pageant. Sharon thought to ask if it was still called the "Christmas pageant" in Sneeds but she didn't, having so much else on her mind that soon crowded out the question. And she began to sense, in their calibrated eagerness to support whatever cockamamie idea she proposed, that the Raths, too, were desperate. Walter apologized for the state's crazy governor, the Trump-before-Trump as he liked to be known.

They were all given the choice. Her idea was met with silence and grumblings and a few jokes and looks, as they sat around after lunch, lazing on a hot day. But when she finally asked for volunteers, of the fifteen participants, eight volunteered. It was the kind of vote of confidence that you get with a night of shooting stars, that seed the heavens with doubt and wonder. These kids, what have they done to me, what have I done to them? Or are they simply doing it *for* me? Go to sleep, my loves, take a nap. The evening will be cool and we'll figure something out then.

Players

She said Luis Espinoza would be in charge of costumes which meant a trip over to the Walmart in Ellsworth. Frank drove the van and had the credit card and kept his opinions to himself. Luis roamed the fluorescent aisles as if they were a passage through the space–time warp, back to indoors and merchandise and Muzak. Not that the Walmart in particular was a place he would shop if he were shopping for himself. He would personally rather shop even on the street than in a place like Walmart. There wasn't a Walmart in the Bronx anyway. You'd have to travel for miles and leave the train behind somewhere and take a bus or walk. All these white people buying cheap and ugly and big. It was something to behold.

Luis, after all, was a connoisseur of more than he was given credit for. He prided himself on his secrets, and wondered if it could have been for the wingtips that Sharon had known he was exactly the man for this job. He started out thinking how when it came to sartorial indications D-Money should differ from Smoothie and Smoothie from Shifty, but soon he went the hundred-eighty-degree opposite direction and felt they should all look alike, because didn't white people see them all alike, Black and brown and it didn't matter whatever else, and shouldn't white people be seeing what white people see, so they can actually *see* what they see? It could have been he had heard that line somewhere, on TV or in a tune. But the problem additionally he was seeing down the fluorescent aisles of the Walmart was the clothes on the racks were entirely too pathetic and lame and low-ball for young citizens of the Borough of Bronx, City of New York, State of New York, pursuers of their drug-drenched dreams up the I-95 corridor, et cetera, even to consider. "Splash of summer!" "Autumnal hues!" And the hoodies were the lamest of them all. No way was he buying hoodies, not if they were all the colors of the Rainbow Coalition. Clichés had their place because everything has its place somewhere, but it wasn't going to be with Luis Espinoza. He began to think it was an important job he was doing, dresser to the stars or holder up of the white-man's mirror to himself.

And then it occurred to him the better thing or the only possible thing would be to buy no costumes at all for D-Money and Smoothie and Shifty, and instead let whoever was going to play their parts wear whatever they were going to wear and only hang around their necks signs that said D-MONEY and SHIFTY and SMOOTHIE in fat magic markers so there could be no mistake, and it would be like a cartoon he felt he'd seen, where that's how you knew who was what and what was who and it was funny except only if you didn't know how to read, which Luis felt with these local people wouldn't be a problem. So he found the correct aisle after going down many that were not, leaving in his wake contrails of Spanish curses, and put magic markers and two large sheets of cardboard in the cart that Frank continued to push around.

Then all that was left were the delicate questions of the white girls who D-Money and Shifty and Smoothie were going to get pregnant and how were you going to know they were white girls and who was going to play them anyway, the last question not being Luis's to worry about, except for sure it wasn't going to be any real white girls. So Luis found his way to the lingerie department where he was viewed with suspicion and where even Frank pushing the cart behind him was viewed with suspicion, and where the only good part was that Walmart didn't have anybody to wait on you, so that it could only be the other customers and the security cameras that were viewing him with suspicion. Big white women looked at him like what was he buying big white padded bras for, and big white socks to fill them up even more with, and they stared at him as well when he held up packages of big white panties in order to decide if they were too much of a good thing or they weren't. True to his nature, Luis didn't easily take offense and as for the few women who left the lingerie department sooner than they were otherwise about to, if the shoe was on the opposite foot he could see their situation.

When they arrived to pay, it was then Frank who was the one more stared at, by the frowning social security type who checked them out, it being Frank's cart and Frank's card. Then they were done. Luis felt that he was a minimalist who had accomplished a delicate mission under less than ideal circumstances. It also pleased him to be spending someone else's money, as he hadn't often had this much to spend on his own.

Markus was assigned the role of the white girl who becomes pregnant and this didn't please him a bit. Sharon thinks I'm a fucking homo, he thought, and looked sullen, and Sharon divined more or less what he thought and said the reason she was choosing him to be a white girl was he was the least looking like a white girl of the lot, because he was so big and masculine. But the others had laughed when he was cast and laughed again when Sharon said he was so big and masculine, and Markus stayed sullen. He asked why Luis couldn't do it instead of himself and Sharon said Luis had other things to do. This was on the stage at the village school where they had gathered for their first rehearsal. It had a musty summer-vacation smell and they had opened all the windows.

Markus asked why they couldn't go get some girls, if they had to have girls, or if there weren't any girls then just not have any girls in the play. Sharon said all through most of history there'd been no actresses and men had played women's parts. Were they all homos then? Markus asked, and Sharon wouldn't answer the question and asked instead if he wanted to leave the production altogether. It quieted the room, which had started to laugh again. But Markus didn't want to leave the production. He found he liked it when Sharon spoke to him, and, as it were, disputed with him. The lady could stand up for herself. So there was that to consider. He said he would stay. He added, however, that he would kick the motherfucking ass of any of the bitch-ass homos in the room who took liberties with him while in the course of his theatrical debut.

A little while later Luis fitted him for his bra and panties. This, too, got laughs, and especially when the bra wouldn't hook because Markus was too broad across the back, so that Luis had to find a piece of old rope and add it to the straps, and then it worked, and the pairs of socks in front then more or less stayed in their respective places. This time Markus found he was less irritated by the laughter. He had begun to realize it was on account of him being a star.

The way Rigoberto thought about it, when Sharon asked for volunteers for doing this play, he had to volunteer because if it wasn't for him telling her about D-Money and Smoothie and Shifty from the text he got from his little sister, there wouldn't be any play to start with, so in a sense it was all his idea and he felt a sense of civic responsibility to be a part of the thing that he started. Let others come with their claims. Then, as it happened, Rigoberto discovered that acting was no more a challenge than getting a free ride on the D train. You looked around, you used the eyes and ears

God gave you, you said what you had to say, and you got off the stage. He was D-Money. So now what was his motivation? If you were so dumbass you could look at his name and not know what his motivation was, you should have been getting off the stage before you even got on it. Sharon asked him what D-Money's home life was like and that was no problem for Rigo either, he just put his own home life in there, even if it was nobody else's business and not worth even mentioning except for his little sister Liddie who was a thousand percent God to him. D-Money had the crooked smile just like himself, and D-Money beat the fare when he was back where he belonged and held the gate open for people in a Robin Hood move just like himself, and D-Money knew right from wrong just like himself, even if he picked and rolled somewhat in that department, just like himself. And giving further consideration to his character, Rigoberto asked himself how hard would it be to get a white girl pregnant when you're a good-looking dude flashing bills around and giving tastes out and just come up from the city in a nice Avis car? Sharon didn't know cars so Rigoberto had to specify, they'd not be driving an Escalade because an Escalade would call police on them like flies to 149th Street but a badass Tesla like the S with the AWD would be just fine and adequate and appropriate. As for the moral of the story, if you asked him what it should be as an actor in this play he was trying to convey, that was easy-peasy as well. Let some of these white dudes get addicted. Let them see what it's like. If you want anything good to come out of a bad situation, you've got to get the white people afflicted first.

When Sharon gave the part of Shifty to Tyrell, she knew he stuttered, so he had to wonder what she was doing. She told him he would only have one line, which would be the thing he told her in the Bronx about wanting to see a Christmas tree that was growing in the ground and not just laying on the sidewalk waiting to get bought like a slave. Tyrell asked her why he should say those words, because he didn't understand how they fit in with going to sell drugs or getting girls pregnant. She said it didn't matter if they fit in or they didn't and he should just say them. She said they were beautiful words. She said when he said them it also didn't matter whether he stuttered or not, she wouldn't care at all, one way or the other, and he could practice it both ways if he wanted to, he could even try to stutter.

Tyrell didn't know how to try to stutter. He either did it or he didn't. But he practiced what he had said about the Christmas tree in his mind and then he went in the woods and practiced out loud so no one would hear. Sometimes he stuttered and sometimes he didn't and he tried to tell himself it didn't matter one way or the other. He kept thinking, too, that she had told him his words were beautiful.

She wrote all of it in a night and knew it wasn't good but she also knew that if it had been good it might have been worse than what it was. It wasn't supposed to be good. What she was less sure about was whether it was supposed to hit people in the face or make them laugh. It was five pages long. She hadn't written anything in ten years but what the hell.

And it was anyway all a bunch of guesses, more a blueprint than a script, all up for grabs. The Raths had a printer and she printed out copies. Good, the Ps have to read something. Then they'd do what was done, they'd workshop, they'd rehearse, they'd argue, they'd *improvise*. Come on, guys, tell me I'm wrong. And they did. It rained for two days and she thanked the heavens. Suddenly the ones who hadn't volunteered wanted to be a part. What else were they going to do on a rainy afternoon, shop for souvenirs in Bar Harbor, buy Indian beads to take home? They could all be in the chorus. There hadn't been a chorus before. But what were they going to sing? She designated herself the Stage Manager, a nod to *Our Town*, this being New England and all, but mostly so she could step in if things got out of hand. No robbing the paying customers, please.

Luis made the signs that would tell who was who, Markus queened a bit in his new self-consciousness and asked for still bigger breasts, Tyrell stuttered very much through rehearsals, Rigoberto argued as a matter both of style and misinterpreted gang affiliation whether D-Money should wear red pants or blue, and Sharon worried. Charley had booked the stage for Friday night and put up signs around Sneeds. Folding chairs were brought from the town hall. Sharon ripped up Tyrell's part and reduced it to three words, to make it a better fit or to give him a better chance or both. Praxis over poetry. Everything in a cocked hat. At night she found herself in bed singing Noël Coward again: "Why Must the Show Go On?".

Sweet Dreams

Rose may have been eighty-six but she couldn't get past the idea that the boys weren't getting any. She and Charley had another of their lunches on the patio and it was almost all she could talk about. Charley would try to steer the conversation off it but Rose would manage to bring it around as if sex were the magnetic north pole. What are they doing, are they masturbating? she asked. There must be whores in Bangor, has anyone snuck them in? Or what if it was like jail and they were picking on the one that Charley said she thought might be gay? In some armies, you know, they regulate the whole thing. Bring the prostitutes right on the base or to the battlefield. Jacques Brel had a song, "Next," did Charley know it? The singer loses his virginity in five minutes in an army whorehouse at the front and it's horrifying, as horrifying, you're led to believe, as the war itself. What a way to go, what a way to start. But it happens, or it used to, before such things became more widely available and amateur. Which brought her to the awkward question of whether there were any girls from Sneeds who might be getting involved with boys from the Bronx. Had Charley seen any signs? Charley, finally getting annoyed, asked what such signs might be. Rose declared her naive. Boys and girls will find a way. No, she hadn't seen any *signs*, Charley finally said, hurt by the old woman's relentlessness. And anyway it's for only two weeks, Charley said. But they're supposed to be two weeks of bliss, Rose said, and added that two weeks in a young man's life is like a year, you have to measure it like a dog's life.

Just as she'd kept the hurtful note from the Tree Committee from Walter, Charley kept all of what Rose said from him, afraid that he would agree with her. She felt surrounded by more than she had bargained for. She tried to change the subject in her mind but it wasn't in the mood to be told what to do. She went swimming in the bay. She cleaned out a closet. When she saw Walter, she talked to him about the play and how Sharon had written five pages. She stayed uneasy. Rose was the friend who had made her feel comfortable in Sneeds Harbor from the first. She had shown it could be done. And as the years went by she had shown how old age could be done, with defiance and brightly colored scarves. Rose wasn't *nice*. But she knew on which side of the bed she'd been born. Charley hated to be on her wrong side, hated to feel she was not as bright as a proper acolyte of Rose Britton's should be. At dinner Walter asked her what was wrong and she said nothing. She might have said, because she thought it, that what was wrong was they hadn't had sex since Stephen died, but she didn't. After dinner they watched another old movie on the streamer that showed them. She fell asleep with her head full of rue. Shortly before daylight she dreamed that she had sex with as many of the boys as she could put faces to, and those she couldn't she dreamed and dreamed until she could, as if she were counting sheep, methodical and a little deadly. She was their whore, she was their Babylon, she was big and capacious and took them on one by one or two by two or as many as wanted to come. Her orifices were theirs, she fucked them all or they fucked her, no boy would be left behind, she refused to wake up until she was finished, and she was happy to give, as she had once been happy to sail the Concordia because Walter wanted her to. She awoke with her mouth full of a salty taste.

Donnie Gets a Ride to Pick Up His Truck

Donnie considered it a bad break and perhaps the Lord's vengeance for his imprudence, and in all events something he'd rather not even discuss with Caryn, that a week after he quit the Raths, the differential went screaming into the night on the Silverado, so that now it sat over with Jerry Coolidge in Manset who when he wasn't drinking was a pretty fair mechanic and figured to be half the price of the dealership. The truck was ready to be picked up and Rine was going that way on unspecified business and offered Donnie a ride. Rine would have given him a ride even if he wasn't headed that way because that's how things were done, but it was good that he was going there anyway, as it put no future obligations on anyone. It was most of an hour to get there and along the way Donnie took note of three five-gallon gasoline cans sitting on the seat and floor in the back of the crew cab and he asked Rine, "You going to go burn down a house?"

"Don't even ask," Rine said.

That was the end of that part of it. Rine wasn't in a talkative mood anyway. In terms of human interaction it was more like a desert caravan with occasional oases. Rine congratulated Donnie for no longer being in the Raths' employment. They did talk, by and by, of Rine's upcoming retirement from thirty years of Department of Transportation service and a few details of his pension, which left Donnie envious and aware of the world's injustices; and also of Trump and what he was up to, the general note there being same-old-same-old, which could be reliably spoken of any political regime; and of these kids from New York City and how in Rine's opinion the town could have invoked *force majeure* or posse comitatus or some such doctrine that emergencies are made for to prevent the whole thing from arising in the first place, as the fire-permit approach had been a joke, no enforcement whatsoever, and as far as anyone knew they could have been out there every night about to burn the woods down the way they used to burn whole neighborhoods down in the Bronx, which you could read about online, just google "South Bronx slash history of" for example. That was as talkative as Rine became. He grimaced a lot and Donnie looked up the road with an elbow out, fearful of deer and Rine's sometimes distracted driving, and in general it was a boring trip. Rine did ask about Kevin once, and whether he'd put in a bid for that big job over in the national park. It seemed to Donnie that Rine might have been angling for a post-retirement career extender. Donnie believed Kevin had put in a bid, but he told Rine he didn't know.

It turned out there had been some gear involvement and the bill for the differential came to seven hundred and change, which made Donnie think again about his recent drop in income. Rine, who'd stuck around to make sure the Silverado ran, told Donnie to forget about it and to keep in mind that he'd done the principled thing, which was more than could be said for certain people from away who could remain nameless because it wasn't worth saying their names and giving them the satisfaction. Donnie asked Rine if he'd heard the latest, tomorrow they were putting on a show and the town was letting them use the schoolhouse. Rine nodded that he'd heard, and he'd heard as well that it was their last night and after that *sayonara*, it's been so good to know you. That was the best part about it, the *sayonara* part. Donnie asked him if he'd heard anything about next year. Rine said he hadn't.

D-Money and Smoothie and Shifty

A Play in One Act

By

Sharon Mason

To Stephen

Cast of Characters

D-Money, *a drug dealer from the Bronx*
Smoothie, *a drug dealer from the Bronx*
Shifty, *a drug dealer from the Bronx*
White Boy #1
White Boy #2
White Boy #3
White Girl #1
White Girl #2
The Stage Manager
Chorus

Location

A Parking Lot Off Interstate 95

SCENE ONE

D-Money, Smoothie and Shifty ENTER from the left. There's no car but it looks like they're in one, clumped together front seat and back. D-Money is driving. Shifty has a sack, rather like Santa's pack. They progress to center stage, as
The Stage Manager ENTERS, strolls on the periphery of the scene.

STAGE MANAGER: You'll have to imagine it, but imagine D-Money and Smoothie and Shifty are driving a Tesla. They'd never drive an Escalade because three young men of color driving an Escalade with New York plates on the I-95 north of where you're ordinarily supposed to find them would be driving to a rendezvous with the jailhouse.

D-Money, Smoothie and Shifty make what appears to be a turn and stop downstage.

D-MONEY: Where the fuck's the white dudes?

SMOOTHIE: They're coming, boss. They're on their way.

D-MONEY: You told 'em, the fucking parking lot?

SMOOTHIE: I told 'em, boss. I told 'em.

D-MONEY: Motherfuckers, always late. *(checks the time on his wrist)* My Rolex says it's ten-thirty-three. White standard time, WST, what bullshit.

SMOOTHIE: It's only three minutes, boss.

D-MONEY: Three minutes is three minutes. *Tempus fugit,* fools! We could be off doing another deal. Miles to go before we sleep.

SMOOTHIE: Here they come now!

Three White Boys and two White Girls ENTER. They, too, appear to be in a vehicle. One of the boys is trailing a carry-on bag.

STAGE MANAGER: If you want to know, it's a Subaru.

WHITE BOY #1: Which one of you dudes is D-Money?

D-MONEY: That be me.

WHITE BOY #1: Hi! I'm Bob. That's Bill. That's Tommy. And these are our hos, Nancy and Susie. *(looking to Smoothie)* And you would be?

SMOOTHIE: Smoothie.

WHITE BOY #1: *(to Shifty)* And yourself?

Shifty glares at him and doesn't speak. White Boy #1 reacts uneasily.

WHITE BOY #1: Well, never mind. Just trying to be hospitable. Up in the country we're friendly folks, we just like to know who …

WHITE BOY #2: *(interrupting)* Shut up, Bobbie. *(to D-Money and others)* So what do you fellas got on offer today?

D-MONEY: Corned beef.

SMOOTHIE: And pastrami.

SHIFTY: And pickles.

WHITE BOY #3: And with mustard?

D-MONEY: The fuck is that? Who said anything about mustard?

WHITE BOY #3: I thought …

D-MONEY: Corned beef!

SMOOTHIE: And pastrami!

SHIFTY: And pickles!

D-MONEY: Technically you'd be correct, dude. You don't customarily serve corned beef and pastrami without mustard, but we're out today. *Capiche? Comprende?*

SMOOTHIE: You ready to order or not?

WHITE BOY #1: Sure, okay. *(he gets out what appears to be a shopping list)* We'll take, uh, six corned beef, eight pastrami, uh, no brisket, either, today? *(he reads D-Money's glare)* Okay, then two extra pastrami.

SHIFTY: And pickles!

WHITE BOY #1: Absolutely, pickles! Lots of pickles. Those ones that aren't too done yet, if you have them.

D-MONEY: New dills.

WHITE BOY #1: Is that what they call them? Groovy.

WHITE BOY #2: I apologize for him. Truly.

SMOOTHIE: No problem.

Under this dialogue, Shifty is pulling wares out of his sack. They look like sandwiches in wax paper marked "P" and "C", only much smaller in size. He puts them all in styrofoam boxes and the boxes in a plastic supermarket throwaway.

Shifty holds the plastic bag while White Boy #3 brings out wads of money from the carry-on.

The exchange is made.

WHITE BOY #1: Pleasure doing business with you fellas.

D-MONEY: Right.

WHITE BOY #1: You know how to get out of here? You don't want to be around after dark, ha-ha.

D-MONEY: Matter of fact … you know where there's a McDonald's at?

WHITE BOY #2: Sure. *(gesticulating)* You go up here, you take a right, a quarter mile, second left, Main Street, then …

D-MONEY: *(interrupting)* How 'bout, do us a favor, you go there, you pick us up some burgers, three Big Macs …

SMOOTHIE: Quarter Pounder with Cheese, Filet-o-Fish, lot of fries, and supersize me some shit.

WHITE BOY #1: You got it. Why not? Sure. C'mon, everybody. Show 'em a little local hospitality.

D-MONEY: Hey, hey, hold your horses, friend. Very kind of you. But no need you take the ladies. Why drive all that way in the hot, smelly car? Big Macs stink up a car bad. We'll take care of 'em.

WHITE BOY #1: Good idea. Okay, hos, you stay.

White Boy #1, White Boy #2, and White Boy #3 EXIT. When they're gone, D-Money, Smoothie, and Shifty smile their smiles, and the girls smile back.

D-MONEY: Now you ladies like to disco?

Under which Shifty runs offstage and returns with a boombox. He presses PLAY and the boombox on his shoulder plays a STRAUSS WALTZ.

D-MONEY: *(to White Girl #1)* May I have the pleasure of this dance?

He begins to waltz with her, around the stage, leading her grandly, all but sweeping her off her feet. After several seconds, however, the dancers and music FREEZE mid-step, as D-Money turns to address the audience directly, in near-Shakespearean elocution:

D-MONEY: Are we not all props in the lives of others?

Dance and music resume. Smoothie joins the dance with White Girl #2. Shifty, acting as DJ, holds the boombox throughout.

STAGE MANAGER: And I'm afraid you know what happens next. Your own governor told you.

The stage darkens. All EXIT. The music dies.

SCENE TWO

White Girl #1 and White Girl #2 ENTER. White Girl #2, the pregnant one, very obviously showing, looks mopier than her friend. They face the audience. The Stage Manager ENTERS, hangs at the periphery.

STAGE MANAGER: He said …

WHITE GIRLS #1 & #2: "Half the time they impregnate a young white girl before they leave, which is a real sad thing because then there's another issue we have to deal with down the road."

A BEAT of silence.

WHITE GIRL #2: It's not fair. None of this real sad thing happened to you.

WHITE GIRL #1: It's just how it is, Suze. Didn't you hear the governor? *Half* of us are going to get pregnant. You're the *half.*

The stage darkens. They EXIT.

SCENE THREE

D-Money, Smoothie, and Shifty ENTER from the right. They appear to be in their Tesla again. The Chorus then ENTERS.

D-MONEY AND SMOOTHIE AND CHORUS: *(singing)*:

In the good old summertime,

In the good old summertime.

The stage darkens. All EXIT to the left.

THE END

No one would have called it a perfect performance. Lines were muffed. The boombox failed to play. Markus punched Rigoberto because Rigoberto pinched his ass. The speeches in unison weren't quite. But the waltz, even without music, was magnificent, as the young men flowed over the stage as if they hadn't learned to waltz in a day. And Rigoberto, as D-Money, mastered the white-man's moves, or the capitalist's moves, or whoever's moves they were that weren't his. And the magic-markered signs around the players' necks got the laughs they were supposed to get. And Tyrell, lovely Tyrell of the stutter and the Christmas tree in the ground, didn't stutter. He believed it was because he tried to. He was terrified to be mocked and humiliated, and he had moments of hating Sharon with all his heart even after she eased his way with fewer words, and moments as well when he would rather have been back in Goshen reformatory than get on that stage, but once he was there and formed in his mind the pih-pih-pih-pih-pih-pih of pickles so that he was sure he would be able to say every one of the pihs, what came out instead, as if it were a cosmic mistake and a joke on him forever, was pickles. And pickles a second time, and pickles a third, it was his only line but at the end of it, thrice blessed, he wished there were more.

The cast all hugged her and gathered around her and if she weren't Sharon they might have lifted her up like the coach after a championship and carried her around the room. Instead Maggie Lassiter brought a dozen white roses from the Hannaford supermarket to the stage and Sharon bent down and cradled them as the actors took their bows, half of which were silly and self-mocking and half of which were as real as young men who had seldom been applauded for anything could make them. The schoolhouse theatre had been three-fourths full. It turned out that much of Sneeds wanted to know what their guests were up to. Charley had been ready to bring the roses up herself but then it seemed more fitting for it to be Maggie, whose store was after all the town's heartbeat, and who had admitted to a late change of feeling. It was a moment of sincerity, a single chime of an uncracked bell. And while it would not have been possible to say that opinion was uniform in the audience, just as it was impossible to say that opinion in Sneeds was ever uniform about anything, nevertheless it appeared there had been more enthusiastic clapping than tepid. They liked the fun made of their governor. They loved the kids waltzing. They liked the corned beef and pastrami as code words for whatever they were code words for and they even seemed to like the chance that they themselves and their views of the wide world had been made fun of, satire making friends among the satirized. Though a few were heard to comment that for a play it seemed rather short, and it was possible as well that more didn't like than liked the girls getting pregnant. Once again there was no Gallup to decide.

People walked afterwards to the reception at the Sneeds Harbor Historical Society. The moon rose orange and the town was serene. The Ps went back to the camp because it was their last night and they needed to pack and a clambake awaited them and most of them preferred not to mix with the townsfolk anyway. What would they say? What would they explain? Wasn't it a little late for all of that? None of the townspeople would miss the reception, however. For most of them it would mean dinner, as the Raths had arranged a spread. Sharon walked over with Walter and Charley, walking between them as if they were escorting her, the queen bee, the celebrated director from away. At the reception everybody thanked everybody. The Raths thanked the town for putting up with their folly and for their support over the hardest year that either of them could imagine. Maggie and Doris Bunting, the oil-and-water couple, thanked the Raths for their better natures and for making Sneeds a better place. The other selectmen thanked Walter in particular for reasoning with their doubts and quibbles. And even Herbert Fallows got in the act, commenting that he had to admit that things hadn't taken the dark turn he feared, and that the Raths, and Sharon, should be complimented for it. Walter, almost despite himself, as if it were an oncoming cold he was resisting, began to feel twinges of his old love for the town. Then it was Sharon's turn to say something.

Charley called her up. She trembled because trembling was as much a part of her gift as outbursts of tears, but as well for what she had just now decided to say. It wasn't that there were all white people in front of her, but that they all seemed to be eating cake. She cleared her throat, she let Charley squeeze her hand, and she waited for the applause to stop so that soon all that could be heard in the room were the ticks of plastic forks on paper plates. Then she began, first with her own litany of thank yous, numerous enough for her to pull out a piece of paper as if it were an awards show, and then, folding the paper away, "You know, of course, where all this started. The play, I mean. I was a little hurt, but more than that I felt the boys were hurt. Not that I'm looking for any pity in saying this. I'm just telling how we got here. It seemed like a response. It seemed like something we could do. And in this regard, I want to stick in a special thanks to Frank Symonson as well. At the heart of it, of course, were the names. Those silly names. I hope I'm not spoiling the comedy by rehashing the history of it all. But come on, really: is there anyone even in this room who didn't get a chuckle from the governor trying to come up with African-American names, African-American *criminal* names? D-Money, Smoothie, Shifty—we couldn't have done it without you, fellas. But those names, there's also something, at least for me, maybe for others who look like me, that stings about them. The reason is, of course, that one of the lightning

144

rods, one of the easy targets, for animus against Black folks in our country is this disturbing pattern we have of naming our kids names that white people would never think to name their kids. White people don't like those names specifically because they sound like Black names, and they don't give people jobs because of those names, and are inclined to think people are criminal or unreliable or stupid on account of those names. So why do African-Americans name their kids Dashawna and DeAndre and Jayvon and so on, seemingly on and on? Pride, for one thing. A desire to avoid names they think of as slave names, to discover names that preceded slave names, that are as if blind to servitude itself, that go backward and forward at once. But also, I imagine, because they find those names beautiful. They look at their beautiful baby and they want to give their baby a name that's just as beautiful. Just like all of you, I'm sure. And there's a reason I'm telling you all this. It's a little more personal, I'm afraid. I was born with one of those names. My mama looked at me and thought I was beautiful and named me Dashawna. And years later when I looked around at the world and saw what was out there and what my chances were and got this scholarship to the Milton Academy, I thought, Dashawna, you are no longer Dashawna, you are henceforth Sharon, and you are going to go places, girl, in this world. So I went to Milton Academy where there were other girls named Sharon and then Mount Holyoke College where I was Sharon and on from there. And my mama accepted it. For awhile I thought maybe she didn't understand, she accepted it but didn't understand why. But she understood why. And I'm pretty sure that *why* hurt her feelings. She still looked at me and saw her beautiful little Dashawna, and was proud of the name she gave me, it expressed all that she could give me, and it wasn't enough. So I feel a little badly about that. No, of course, more than a little badly. And so, for a long time, I was wondering who I could ever tell about it. I suppose I can thank D-Money and Smoothie and Shifty for giving me this chance. And all of you."

Then she walked quickly into the crowd in front of her, so that when she cried there would be the soft fabric of the lives of others to stanch her tears.

Last Night

It was the last night and so after the reception Walter and Charley went out to the camp. Sharon had gone on earlier. They parked on the inbound drive and crossed the field with a flashlight. They might have been gleaning or looking for something lost. On the pebble beach where the clambake had been, there was now a bonfire burning. A light breeze kept it lively. The kids were quaffing champagne and downing oysters and toasting marshmallows. Previously they'd had their own little championship season and sprayed one another with champagne fizz so that now their clothes were sticky. They didn't seem to mind. Clouds just now covered over the moon. Walter was tipsy from the reception where he had drunk out of relief. It was all coming to a close. Disaster had been averted. A kind of Platonic harmony had prevailed. Or was it a Ptolemaic harmony? He was too tipsy to be sure. The natural order, once out of joint, now restored, wait wait don't tell me, who that was, what that was, if that was.

The Raths stood at the periphery. The kids paid them no mind. When Frank approached, Walter took him aside.

"Did you get a permit?" he asked.

"Oh shit," Frank said.

"Just be sure it's out," Walter said.

Now the kids took note of their company. "Yo, Walt!" one shouted.

And another, "Yo, Charley!"

"Have some of this fizzy shit, man!"

"Got no manners, fuck?"

"He apologizes."

"Good time here, bro."

"Be missing you."

And like that, a little while. One of them had a bottle and sent some froth their way. Charley brushed it from her eyes and smiled. It occurred to Walter, somewhere in the sea of kumbaya, that they, his guests, had gotten through two weeks without women or drugs. At least as far as he knew. Then it occurred to him that they would have been trained for that in reform school or jail. A two-week bit.

Once the fire was out and the Ps were to their cabins, Frank was to stop by Sharon's cabin for a nightcap and good-byes. He arrived as if bearing offerings, an extra Moët from the clambake and the weed that was always with him. He also carried the fire extinguisher he'd borrowed to be sure every ember would be out. It was past eleven and the air felt funny, as if something was blowing in. Sharon had been growing impatient for him to arrive. She was planning to be up at six.

When he did get there, he was as awkward as he could be, which might have been a signal, but if so of what? He put the extinguisher down and offered her his dope, which she declined with an offhand wave. She may have been facetious or only playful when she said it would set a bad example. They popped the champagne and toasted with plastic cups the intersectionality of the world. This too could have been facetious or only playful. It was the one thing Frank had left to sell, if you looked at it that way. His hopes for the world, his blurry optimism that scarcely believed in itself but held to the proposition regardless, because what would people do all day if they simply gave up? Or, correction, perhaps: what would Frank do all day? He dared not speak for others, he said. Had not his people too often done exactly that, spoken and preached and ordered? Sharon asked him if there weren't some circularity there. If his people had preached and ordered too much, why was he preaching and ordering *intersectionality* now? She was arguing with him because that too was a facetious or perhaps only a playful thing to do. And because he was slightly zonked and she wasn't, she could out-argue him and he would neither notice nor take offense. It was like playing handball with herself. This was the father of a boy she had once been a little fond of, half a lifetime before Stephen, a boy who had even awed her, who had everything when she had little, yet his father didn't frighten her at all.

They sat in their respective camp chairs and poured a bit more champagne when their glasses were low and talked about Peter and the Philippines and the big oil companies and the planet and Strindberg and the Ps and whether a good time had been had by all and Sharon thanked him again for D-Money and the rest and he praised her stage direction and her writing and all-round talent and so they got by most of an hour saying hardly anything at all. There were mosquitoes and occasionally she swatted at them ineffectually while Frank didn't bother. A breeze had come up and was batting the windows with soft breaths of the night.

"You know what I want to see someday?" she said. "That place you saw in Africa."

"What place?" he said.

"Oh, come on, you can't be too stoned to remember that. The ruins, the city."

"Oh, that," he said, and smiled, because it was something he was fond to remember.

"Did it have a name?" she asked.

"I don't know," he said. "If it did, I never knew it."

And each must have thought they could google it and find the name, but each must have felt, as well, that by the time they googled it and found it they would have spoiled the reason for her asking.

"I'd like to go there someday," she said. "I'd like to see it for myself."

"You'd love it," he said. "It would be like a dream."

"I thought it might be a little like the woods here," she said. "With the old hotel, the ruins."

"Much grander," Frank said.

"Of course. Much grander," she said.

By then he had seen the slender fall of her neck down from the puffs of her hair and the shape of her breast under the clean loose broadcloth of her shirt and the quickness of her eyes and the way her tongue clicked her teeth when she said certain words and thus he was almost prepared to forget that she was not even his son's age and perhaps had had a crush on Peter once, and he was prepared also to forget that he himself was decrepit and probably impotent, though you never could be sure about the last part, it was one of those mysteries that time forgot; and, though he hadn't forgotten the chance that Sharon was yet getting over a lover, Frank was one who believed in both past and present, who lived in their roiling back-and-forth seas, who saw them as one even when they resisted. So he got up from his camp chair and hovered over her because he was very tall and she laughed because he was hovering and he looked puzzled and hurt because she was laughing, which made her laugh the more.

Sharon felt some sadness then. Sometimes the world would have to go on its way. "I didn't think this was a date," she said.

Then her phone rang. A few seconds later, his rang. Then there was rapid knocking on the door. There was a fire.

The Ps were safe. Everyone was safe. Fire departments from five towns around responded. The fire was erratic, taking this field and not that one, these stands of trees and not those. Two of the cabins burned and much of the Raths' field, but the wind shifted and the volunteers raced to the other end of the woods to try to save the houses there. Frank and Sharon rounded the Ps up and drove them to the village and parked them at the town hall. Sneeds seemed stripped of its males. It was briefly like a war. Nearly breathless, with a jacket thrown over his nightshirt, Walter went out with the rest to the end of the woods where the houses were. But three of them were lost. Then it rained and things calmed down. Recriminations could wait until morning.

Fire Is a Dangerous Thing

The first thing on Walter's agenda the following day was to find Frank, but it was hardly necessary because Frank found him. Neither had slept much. A smoky haze lingered over the village, so that the morning felt hardly like morning at all, a hangover in the clouds. It is not the easiest thing for old friends to confront hard truths. "Have you smoked this morning?" was the first thing Walter asked, as Frank's eyes looked dilated or were anyway like little red stones.

But Frank said he hadn't and that his eyes, however they were, were only from lack of sleep.

"And what about last night?"

They were out by the curb, where Walter had put the trash out. He had his car keys in his hand and he turned them like worry beads.

"You know. The normal," Frank said. "Look ..." He calmed his upper lip with his teeth. His eyelids flicked without intention. "I screwed up. Okay? Screwed up royally. Sorry, Walt. Couldn't be sorrier."

Walter nodded, eyes averted, more in embarrassment than anger, because it was something to hear such a confession from a friend.

"You hired me. You depended on me," Frank went on.

"Shut up. Forget it."

"But I'll say one thing. I knew about the permits. I should have gotten one. Should have every night. Just was lazy or thought it was bullshit. But ... I don't know how it happened. I followed every ember. I dowsed everything. It was dead. Hey, it's not like I don't know fires."

"Merit-badge Frank," Walter said without sarcasm.

"You look like you're going to sneeze," Frank said.

"More like a smile," Walter said. "Manly efforts to suppress a smile."

"You always had a sick sense of humor," Frank said.

"I don't know about that," Walter said.

"It was dead," Frank said.

"Embers and dope," Walter said. "And a breeze."

"You're saying you don't believe me," Frank said.

"I am," Walter said.

"I'm not sure I believe myself," Frank said.

The selectmen's special meeting was called for three. Before it even began, Walter had consulted with a lawyer in Bangor but the lawyer said there was nothing to be done for now. Or not exactly nothing, unless admitting nothing is nothing. Walter regretted making the call. It made him feel cheap, and as if he had lost a portion of his autonomy. They tell you what to do even when they don't. He called the insurance company as well. This was more pro forma, reporting the incident because it was required. By 2:45 the meeting room was full to overflowing. There were even a few curious tourists, hoping to observe old-fashioned direct democracy in action. Charley did not attend. She was distraught, most especially and recently because Rose Britton had phoned just before lunch to say that the chickens had come home to roost, that it was all so predictable, and that if you live in a small town you have to consider it like a single human being, with feelings to consider and instincts to acknowledge. It was the last that hurt the most, because to Charley it made too much sense, the cruel crack of enlightenment, the Zen master's stick.

Lawyers be damned, Walter opened the meeting with an

apology. Both in tone and substance it borrowed from Frank's. The largest difference was that he didn't claim the bonfire was out. He claimed only that Frank thought it was out. "I accept full responsibility and I invite full scrutiny. Let's get the adjusters out here, or the marshals, or whoever it is, and get an official report. The only thing I ask, pending investigation, of course, is that people don't go around and start blaming these kids. From all we know now, they had nothing to do with it. They're leaving tonight. Some of them may already have been a bit traumatized. I beg all of you, let's leave them with whatever happy memories they can take away from their time here." He sipped his bottled water and surveyed the room. "I don't see Jerry and Kit Marsden, or Mike Devereaux, or Sally and Paul Eichley, are any of you ..." But they weren't there. "Anyway, I called them all, it's terrible, horrible, we're doing what we can for them, while their housing needs are assessed. I'm afraid the preliminary is the Marsdens, they're facing a teardown. You can imagine how Charley and I feel about this. That's all I have to say for the moment."

Walter hardly felt bathed in the bath of mercy, but at least he had had his say. They could believe him or not, trust him or not, and it would still be all his fault, just as earlier it had all been Frank's. Selectman Cummings then opened the room for questions and discussion. The surprise was how few had anything to say. It was as if they were sitting on hallowed ground. It was hardly the first fire in Sneeds history, the woods had burned many times, but this time felt premeditated, or inevitable, or as though it simply shouldn't have happened. It was left to Herbert Fallows to say anything at all. "I'm glad the sheriff's here," he said. He looked towards the back, where a fresh-faced red-headed deputy, whose appearance could have suggested to any number in the room the wisdom that you know you're old when the cops look young, was standing behind the last row of folding chairs. "Because what nobody's talking about, but there has to be a criminal investigation. Has to be."

"Could you elaborate a little, Herb?" Selectman Cummings asked. "Not sure where you're going with this."

"Perfectly obvious. We make a law. The law's violated. Bad things happen as a result."

"But I don't see where the facts are in dispute here," Selectman Roberts said.

"No, they're not. So what are we going to do? Sit here like ninnies, like nothing happened? That's how you get disrespect for the law, that's how you get crime waves."

"Oh, come on, Herb," Cummings said.

"All I'm saying, it's a matter of respect. And self-respect. It shouldn't be a fifty-dollar fine."

"Nobody's talking about a fifty-dollar fine," Roberts said. "But why get the sheriff involved? There's an implication there."

"I already called the sheriff. I filed a complaint."

"Point of order. Does he have standing to file a complaint?" Harry Casey asked from a seat on the aisle.

"That would be for the sheriff to consider, not us," Selectman Roberts said.

"So point of order denied?"

"Point of order not a proper point of order. Denied."

"I warned of consequences like these. It looked like we were in the clear. I should have listened to myself," Herbert said. "And I'll just mention one thing more. In the course of fighting the fire, a large quantity of alcohol was found on the premises of the Whitlock camp. Now I don't suppose there's eyewitness evidence beyond those who would cite the Fifth Amendment to prove a charge of serving beverages to minors, but it doesn't diminish that it was in all likelihood happening."

Walter had not wanted to say more; rather, he had wanted the town to have its say. But it was plain that Herbert was goading him. Finally he felt goaded, as though asked to dance so sincerely that he could finally hardly decline.

"You want me to quit, Herbert, is that what it is? You think I should resign?"

"I think you should recuse yourself from the matter, at minimum. Yes, recuse yourself," Herbert said.

"I'll do you one better. I quit," Walter said.

It was precipitous and got the room's attention and for a few moments silenced even Herbert. Walter didn't know where it came from, but it must have been lurking there all along and he could hardly deny it now. It felt oddly like a pledge of good faith. You resign and if they really want you, they take you back with arms glad or twisted, but still they take you back.

But they didn't take him back. A stunned silence of having broken the sound barrier prevailed. Finally Selectman Cummings asked, "You sure, Walter?"

"Why not?" Walter said. He looked out at the room of people he'd known, a lot of them, twenty-five years, and some others whose parents he'd known. "How many here think it's the right thing I resign from the Board of Selectmen? Be honest. You're my friends. You heard my apologies and regrets, you can take them for sincere or not. But, please, give me an honest count. You've seen the devastation. It's not only in property, it's personal too. Fire is a dangerous thing."

There could have been a parliamentary move to stop the count, but nobody raised a hand or called this time for a point of order. There was more, instead, of that silence where something is out-raced. "Hands, please?" Walter asked. "The right thing?"

A few hands went up, then more, like a rain starting, and soon it was raining hands.

By the time Walter asked if it was the wrong thing, there

weren't as many hands left to be raised. Roughly speaking, the vote was three to one. This time the town parted its hair on the side. Walter walked out feeling a certain satisfaction. For once he felt sure of something.

When Charley was finally exhausted with blaming herself, she blamed Frank. But her mind was running like a fuse of dynamite and it wouldn't stop until it got to Walter. Why had he hired Frank in the first place? She had her guesses and she said them all. Because he was too trusting, too sentimental, too weak when it came to friends and too willing to put his friendships in front of their marriage. Because he'd never got past the lure of Yale and all that shit. Because he was still playing the Jew and somehow imagined that Frank was still playing the WASP. Because he was a gambler with their fortune and Frank was not the first bad bet. Because why had they ever come to Sneeds in the first place, except out of some fantasy she never shared? She'd gone along, so she blamed herself too. If they'd done anything differently, if they'd done even one thing differently, wouldn't Stephen still be alive?

Walter absorbed it all because he was too tired and wounded not to. She didn't seem to give a damn if he quit the selectmen or not or even if he was pushed. He decided she was probably right. When she was enraged, she was usually right. This, too, reflected the properties of fire. They were downstairs and he had fixed her tea but by now the tea was cold. Where he finally ran out of patience, or whatever it was, was when she talked of Stephen still being alive.

She was curled on the couch. He had been slowly pacing, taking in the carpet's patterns as if they led somewhere. "And if Stephen were alive, we wouldn't have had these kids up here, and if the kids hadn't been here, there wouldn't have been the fire, and if there hadn't been the fire we wouldn't be here tearing each other apart."

"We're not," she said. "I'm tearing you apart."

"Correction accepted."

"Don't try to trick me," she said.

"All I mean is, life goes on."

"Now there's a strikingly original thought."

"It's not, is it? But then why are we trying to stop life in its tracks?"

"You mean me? Why don't you just say me?"

"Correction once again accepted."

"I hate these quibbles. Just yell and scream."

"Would you like me to refresh your tea?"

"No, thanks."

Then Walter might have screamed. It was in his throat and heart. He said instead, "I'd call you a name right now, but why give you the satisfaction?"

"A body part, maybe? Something along those lines?"

"Please, Charley, just stop it."

"Go on. Give it a shot. Yell and scream."

But he didn't. He'd never been the type and it seemed he wasn't about to start, as if a chalk circle were drawn around him.

"What a gallant coward you are," she said.

"It's an unlovely name," he said.

Nothing much of significance was said after that.

Assessments

Markus hadn't a doubt that he was the one who got the big-time laughs. There was Rigo, of course, with his D-Money hustle, acting like a fifty-dollar pimp, prancing around, dancing around, but such comparisons offended Markus's new-found dignity. Was it not apparent to any fair-minded person that it was Markus's tits that got the laughs? Markus being pregnant, that one too, the way those white folks were laughing. Though Markus reminded himself not even to think "white folks," it could have been any folks if you were six feet four with tits that needed a rope to tie them on, people were going to laugh their asses off. In the Suburban on the way to the airport, Frank said to all of them they might want to take a few minutes to reflect on their time there and what worked and what didn't and to feel free with their criticisms, so that was exactly what Markus was doing, in his opinion, in his head, making the proper assessments. As soon as Sharon got to be a big-time director downtown, he intended to give her a call and remind her of the laughs he got. And from there he could go places, he could go as far as he could see, so that you couldn't even see him from the Bronx. Markus reflected on the number of supersize Mr. Clean-types who'd become stars just like that. He could play a genie in a bottle. He imagined himself the first Black Frankenstein, or the next Black Frankenstein, or whatever that would be. And at that point they could say he was as dumb as they wanted to, but the only laugh would be on themselves. Markus was not unaware that he was letting his mind run fantastically, but he decided for a little while, on the bus, and still a long way from home, to let it run.

As for the worst part of the two weeks, the part he would advise in the strongest terms they avoid in the future, that would be the fire. The fire felt evil to Markus, as if they had all been touched by a demonic hand. He had been asleep like it was Sunday morning glide time, all packed up to leave the next day, when suddenly Tyrell was shaking him, g-g-g-get up et cetera, though in retrospect Markus wasn't sure if Tyrell had stuttered then or not, it was all so sudden and surprising, smoke everywhere and flames too, flames right at the end of the cabin. If it wasn't for Tyrell waking everybody up, who knows what could have gone down? Markus grabbed his phone and ran out the other end and at first he'd felt pleased with himself that at least he'd saved his phone but later he learned that those who lost theirs were going to get repaid and probably wind up with new ones. This was now causing Markus a serious bout of phone envy, such that he was considering saying his too went up in the flames. As they drove to Bangor he could see a new iPhone Plus in his future. One other good part amid the bad, in Markus's estimation, was Tyrell himself, who for a skinny dude who talked as inadequate as he talked, did some brave deeds, waking everybody, shaking everybody, barely getting his own self out in the end.

Luis Espinoza sat in the waiting room of the Bangor airport and found his thoughts drifting in the direction of the Raths' woods. His feelings were hurt that they were all burned down or most of them were anyway. He'd liked walking in there. It could have been the first place he'd ever been where nobody could come around and bother him. He could walk in as far as he wanted and nobody else would even come close. Way back there, way away from everybody, he even found a part that seemed to have once had human habitation, like there were two ancient bathtubs turned upside down, and it was right next to those bathtubs that Luis saw a deer.

He didn't tell anyone about the deer, because who would care? The white people, for one, saw deer all the time. All he heard them do was complain about them. But the deer he saw, saw him back, with a kind of sidewise eye, and it just stood there, so that Luis had been afraid to move—even if he swallowed, would the deer hear him swallow and run away? So in his memory that was the best part, the deer and its sideways eye. He was a little embarrassed even to think like that, like what kind of person was that, who never saw a deer before? He'd been so afraid it would run away that he didn't even take his camera out. But he knew he would always remember it. He even knew it would be better to remember it than to have a stupid picture. The deer ran away on its own. Who could say what reason a deer could have? Luis thought about the deer and thought about the fire. Was it just like Bambi? He couldn't remember exactly, Bambi or Bambi's mama, but somebody died in that, for sure. He hoped the deer didn't die.

Nothing about the rest of the time could compare. The eats, the Moe-Ett and what not, everything off the top shelf, the play, the boat, the golf club, et cetera, et cetera, not even the whole thing with the ice cream cone and Jayden and his sarcastic tone. Nobody could say those people, the Raths, didn't try. Really, he ought to write a thank you, Luis thought. Maybe he would, maybe he would send a text, *muchas gracias, compadres*, something along those lines, a gesture, really, of equality, like the Bronx knows how to behave as well as anyone.

In the morning, after the fire, Luis had gone back out to the woods, and the trees that he had begun to love looked like a lot of black sticks, like they were just stuck in the ground. You could almost think that the woods were like back home. Everything can burn, everything beautiful can be gone. That was one thing he didn't really have to learn. But he had seen the deer, and he could remember it, and so, Luis imagined, as long as he saw it and remembered it, it wouldn't be really one hundred percent gone. Not until he died too. And then maybe somebody would remember him, and the whole thing would get carried on, like a little bit of him would be in the somebody who remembered him and still a littler bit of the deer would be in the little bit of him. Crazy thoughts, crazy days. But sitting there waiting for the plane, they made him a little happy.

What Tyrell was thinking about in the waiting room was Sharon. It was to the point where the one thing he was aware of in a room was whether she was in it or not, and she wasn't. He imagined maybe the TSAs had held her up. Or she lost her ID. What if her ride had an accident, or what if she just decided on another course of action and wasn't coming home at all? If she was coming home, of course, he could see her while going around on his business, once a week even, when he went in for his appointment. She could be around the office and he'd just run into her. Or he could look around the court. You can look around the court, they can't arrest you for that, it's a free country would be his defense if anybody like one of the court officers said what the fuck are you doing around here, Tyrell.

The waiting room of the airport was like detention itself. Time enough to consider all the worst-case scenarios, like if it turned out in fact she was gone, if she just decided she liked all the Christmas trees up here and said bye-bye to the Bronx and all its problems, could he see himself coming back to look for her? How that might work exactly, Tyrell wasn't too sure. Take the bus, maybe hitch a ride. *Hey, dude, you headed north?* Not a high-percentage play, he would have to estimate. Call up those people then. *Yo, Charley, you seen where Sharon's at?* But what would he say if he found her? Tyrell guessed that he would probably start stuttering again.

He was having such thoughts mixed in a confusing soup of others, like should he go to the bathroom before he got on the plane because he couldn't remember if they even had a bathroom on the plane, and more especially he had no intention to get out of his seat once he was on there, no way he would be taking his seatbelt off and get sick again, not till they were safe and sound on the ground at LaGuardia airport looking right over at the familiar rock of Rikers, which in this case would feel like an island of stability. But he decided not to use the facilities at the moment because he was looking around to see about Sharon.

Then he could see her through the glass at the TSA picking up her bag and so on, putting on her shoes, and then she came into the waiting room, and went into the place where you get the candy and magazines. Tyrell imagined himself going over there to get a pack of gum himself. He had a couple of singles in his pocket, he could pretend to be browsing around, *Hey, Sharon, would you favor the Starbursts or what have you?* Or could he come right out and announce, in a casual manner of course so it wouldn't come out like a brag, had she heard how he saved the other boys in the fire? Tyrell mocked himself then. No way he was doing anything like any of that. It would be one more time when he would probably start stuttering.

Then she came out with a newspaper. Who goes in the airport and buys a newspaper and no candy? Sharon, that's exactly who. His eyes followed her around. First she talked to a couple other of the Ps, just saying hello or things of that nature, nothing to get crazy jealous and cranked off about or consider why it wasn't himself she was coming up to, then she sat down with her newspaper. Soon after, they started calling people to the plane. He hoped by some chance it would turn out he was sitting right next to her. Now wouldn't that be the Lord's grace! Tyrell felt for a moment the light-headedness of someone who could still believe in dreams. Then he watched her from behind as they stood in the line to get on the plane. He thought what difference would it even make if he sat next to her and stuttered, she was the one who told him to try to, that was how he fell in love with her in the first place.

Rigoberto Colon's report card on his two weeks in Sneeds Harbor, Maine, would be as follows:

For the rib-eyes, A.

For the hot-fudge sundaes and especially for having them for breakfast if you wanted, A.

For the lobsters, which once you had a few of them and started knowing how to take them apart were still messy shit but tasted good, B+.

For the lack of females, F.

For the lack of controlled substances, D, which would have been an E or an F if he hadn't found a dude in Ellsworth to help him out a little in the weed department.

For the boat, and in particular for the fact that it tipped this way then that way and in addition for the fact which he'd been informed of that with the water temperature in that vicinity being what it was, once you fell off the boat, you froze to death in five minutes or less even if you didn't drown, C-.

For Sharon, A.

For the fire, F.

For his man Frank, who was pretty chill throughout but in particular drove them to Ellsworth and pointed the way to where the individual with the weed could be found, A-.

For Charley because first off she was a good looker for her years, the woman knew how to keep in proper condition, but secondly the way she was always coming around, asking questions, fixing things, wanting to help Sharon, and even with all that cash she had on hand what did she drive, a little electric thing, which just showed she wasn't into showing off, A-.

For Walter, who was good, but who didn't appear to care about the boys as much as Charley did, possibly because he could have had certain other things on his mind all the time, B+.

For the town itself being a beauty, A, but for its overall friendliness that seemed like it could come and go, like at the play, definitely yes, but at the end with the fire, definitely and outstandingly not, which by the way he could understand, insofar as if it was his own house that burned down, he'd be pissed as shit, C+.

For the promise to replace all the burned-up phones and laptops and what not and help get your data back, A.

For the steel-drum band they had to listen to for about fourteen hours, E.

For the oysters, clams and mussels which in his personal opinion were a little on the gooey side of the culinary universe, B.

For the pie ladies who made all the good pies, A.

For the weather that wasn't too bad, not sticky-on-your-balls like all the time in the city, B.

For the mosquitoes and ticks they were always telling you about, like to watch your clothes and put your pants in your socks, which as a matter of fashion was not a good look, C-.

For the day they went in the kayaks and got wet and cold, B-.

For his fellow Ps, brown or Black or whatever didn't matter, up here it was like they were all from one big neighborhood, A.

For the amount of overall fun these white people had doing all that they were doing, C.

And finally and not least, no comparison, hands down, A+++, best performer in a dramatic presentation goes to Rigo Colon himself for his outstanding character of D-Money in the stirring play by Sharon Mason about what goes down in this world. *Are we not all props in the lives of others?*

An Email Sharon Received While Waiting
in the Baggage Claim at LaGuardia

Frank Symonson
Re: a P.S.
To: Sharon Mason
P.S. Sharon, hi, just wanted you to know one thing. Was going to tell you the other night. Guess I was looking for the right moment & maybe it was a slightly tender thing & then of course things got a little hectic. I knew you were Dashawna. I knew it from when I talked to Peter. And I understand how you'd feel about all of it, and I guess I've got to say sorry for being the kind of person you'd want to change your beautiful name for. But it is beautiful. So is Sharon. Take your pick, I say. When I'm in the city, can I give you a call? xF

So there was that too to consider. All those years at Milton and nobody ever said a word. She tried to remember if there had ever been even undeciphered looks, looks that at the time she might have taken as looks to her Blackness, but that had this added coda, this questioning of something laid over her Blackness or perhaps underneath her Blackness. But she couldn't. What exquisite *politesse*, what well-brought-up folks. It was like a farce uttered in silence. Secrets make more secrets. She couldn't tell if she was angry at him or relieved for him telling her. But she knew she would never see Frank Symonson again. Her bag came down the chute, she said good-bye to some of the boys, and went out to get a cab.

Considerations

Once in a while Donnie and Kevin met up at the Canterbury when there was some father-and-son stuff to be considered, or if you would be less charitable you could call it man-talk, Sunday suppers being even after the casseroles and pies were finished off generally unsuitable for that purpose, in that you could walk a hundred yards down the road and somehow the women would still get their antennas up and their opinions into the discussion and more often than not wind up with the last word. Kevin was never the drinking sort, and more especially in his years of marriage and becoming a church-going Catholic like Mary Louise his bride, but half a beer once in a while wasn't going to hurt him and Donnie had texted him to say he'd appreciate it if they could meet up. Kevin was fearful that his dad was going to ask him for money. He knew that since he quit the Rath job, money had become a question mark. His reluctance wasn't on account of any stinginess on Kevin's part, who several times in the past years had been there to help out, and actually been happy to have the chance to show how life had worked somewhat in his favor, but just at the moment he was in some straights himself, with a lawsuit over on Mount Desert concerning some trees that fell on a garage and his liability insurance jacking his rates sky high in consequence, and in addition Loozie facing some surgery that another insurance company was calling optional when there was no way it was optional, not if you had half a heart still beating in your pissant insurance-adjuster chest.

Donnie was waiting when he got there. He had a heavy look, his whole forearms leaning on the bar, and Kevin didn't like the look of it. "Hey, Pops," and so on.

They talked about the Sox awhile. The ball game was on but the sound was off. Donnie peeled the label on his beer and finally paid the ball game no mind. They were losing anyway. "You hear about the fire?" Donnie asked.

"Of course I heard about it. I talked to Mom this morning."

"Right down the road. Five more houses, could have been us."

"No, I heard. Bad news. I heard Kit and Jerry lost theirs whole."

"It's what they're saying."

"And it was some bonfire shit did it. Jesus! How could they not get the permit even? You were still working there, you wouldn't of allowed that, would you?"

"No way," Donnie said.

"The Raths ... I don't know. Probably you're just as well out of there. I know it cost you. You doing okay, Pops? The money situation's okay?"

"It's okay."

"So what's going on?" Kevin asked, somewhat relieved, as Donnie picked his label clean and kept his eyes away and offered a very nearly undetectable shrug, like he was flicking away a speck of dust.

"You hear anything else? I mean about the fire?" he asked Kevin.

"Not really."

"Everybody's saying it's the Raths, it's those kids, right?"

"I haven't talked to 'everybody.' I don't know. Why? You hear something different?"

"Uhn-uh. Uhn-uh. Nothing different."

"Then what?"

"Just a hunch, maybe."

"Not sure where you're headed with this, Pops."

"Ah, fuck it! Just fuck it!" Donnie clenched his fists and Kevin waited to see if there'd be more.

But there wasn't, so finally Kevin said, "You know until this happened, I was happy the thing happened, I mean, the whole thing, the camp, all those kids. I was happy they did it. I mean, why not? It was something for Stevie. It made me remember him."

"That's good," Donnie said.

"It *was* good," Kevin said. "Don't know about now."

Donnie then considered his options, and why it was in the first place he'd asked Kevin to meet him. It wasn't so he could pull off beer labels. And the thing about Kev, he was a good boy. He'd always been a good boy and he even gave pretty fair advice, nor did he hold it over you afterwards. It was one thing Donnie could be proud of, actually, how Kevin turned out, and the kids in turn, he and Loozie, they were doing their job the right way with the kids.

So he said, "Just hypothetically, Kev, if you had some information about something, but it was pretty vague, but at the same time it was something, it wasn't just like you're making it up in your head, but also at the same time it could involve an individual happens to be someone you know, so you could get that someone in a spot even if they didn't do anything, maybe they'd have to explain themselves, maybe they'd have to go get a lawyer and all of that, it could cost them ... would you?"

"Would I what?"

"Don't be dense now. Report 'em. To the whoever, the sheriff."

"Depends," Kevin said. "We're talking about the fire now?"

"We are."

"And we're talking about ..."

"Shall remain nameless. Until innocent is proven guilty."

173

"But were they negligent, or did they do something deliberate? You're talking about the Raths now?"

"I am not."

"Somebody who had something against the Raths? Doing something against the Raths?"

"What is this, twenty fucking questions?"

"As I recall, it was you brought the subject up."

"Then just forget it. It's not necessary. I'll figure it out myself."

"Okay ... As you wish, Pops ... But offhand I'd say, if somebody did something deliberate against somebody, something really harmful, doesn't matter who it was ..."

"And if it was me who did it and you who knew something ..."

"That's not what you're saying, is it, Pops?"

"Unh-uh. Unh-uh. Just by way of example."

"Maybe blood relations are a little different."

"Point well taken."

Kevin, too, was tiring of the twenty questions. His father had always been a man who hoarded up his words, he would fill up every room of his house with unuttered words, you couldn't even open a door with so many words piled up. The splurge now seemed like nothing but confusion. "Somebody set the fire, Pops? Somebody you know?"

But Donnie wasn't saying. "I told you this in confidentiality," he said. "And nothing's for sure."

"I understand that," Kevin said.

It seemed time to pay a little more attention to the ball game. Overhead the Sox were rallying, guys were crossing the plate. If the middle relief didn't blow it as usual, maybe they'd pull this one out. Donnie was reminded of when Kevin played the American Legion ball or one of those, and the team he was on was the Red Sox. It was like always rooting for the home team, something you could be certain about, as opposed to the situation he now found himself in.

What he didn't mention to Kevin was this whole business about the white race going down the tubes. He didn't mention it in part because Kevin wasn't going to have much appreciation of it, now especially with Loozie being so good and so on, but in addition he himself, Donnie, had lost some of his appreciation. It was only relevant now as to what on the crime programs they would call motivation. Did Rine have the motivation or didn't he? Because of his hanging around with a bunch of screw-loose types, you could say definitely. Did Rine have the means? Donnie saw it with his own eyes. Did Rine make threats in that area? Well, maybe, possibly, open to interpretation. Donnie tried to imagine it the other way, the sparks flying from the bonfire into the grass and it going on from there. Could be, could be, would have never happened on his watch, as Kevin was right to point out, but maybe. On the other hand, it was a ways from the beach to the woods. Wouldn't've somebody seen something before fire made it to the woods?

Donnie drove home from the Canterbury in a state. He found himself not wanting to disappoint Kevin. Not that he was sure which course of action would disappoint him or not, nor did he have reason to believe Kevin would even find out. But here, too, was a question of blood. He was in Kevin's veins but just as much wasn't Kevin in his? Donnie wasn't sure how it would work, especially with that kind of reversal, having to run upstream as it were, but if there was one thing he had faith in, it was that. It wasn't in the white race, that was for sure. Just call it a lost cause. All those chat rooms, all those raving ass-sniffers. If they were ever in one real room, they'd probably chop one another up pretty good. Donnie didn't pride himself on being any genius, but he did feel you could count on him for a no bullshit, commonsensical approach. It was enough to worry about Cormer blood, he wasn't going to worry about all the blood of all the losers in the world. Halfway home to Sneeds, he turned around and drove back Route 1. It didn't feel so much that he'd decided anything as that his hands and arms on the wheel and his foot on the gas just took him there.

In Ellsworth was the last working pay phone he knew about anywhere in the county. He turned off his own phone before he got there so there wouldn't be any of that location-tracking business you couldn't help but be reading about every other day. Then he phoned the sheriff's office and said without giving his name or anybody else's name for that matter that they really ought to be looking in the woods regarding that fire over in Sneeds, for the possibility of arson being involved, with an accelerant or something of that nature, as there may have been some individual out there looking to do the Rath family and their project with the juvenile delinquents harm. He left the phone booth fairly quickly, as he wasn't sure of the capacity of the sheriff's department to track down that particular location, and drove home. In the aftermath, when all was said and done, he felt he had taken a no-bullshit approach, made a commonsensical compromise. If it was Rine, it was Rine, but he wouldn't be the one who said it. As for Walter and Charley, white people or otherwise, they'd always been pretty good to him and that had to be taken into account.

Hate Crime

By the second day the woods were full of men. It was almost like hunting season. The sheriff's department had notified the fire marshals and there were investigators from both those offices and the Raths' insurers had sent a team as well. They all fanned out and it was scarcely mid-afternoon before they found traces of gasoline leading from the Clarkswood Road down one of the old carriage tracks and only stopping where you came in the vicinity of the hotel ruins, as if a fire from one time had begotten a fire in another. Around the Nazareth there was more evidence of acceleration. At this point the sheriff determined that the FBI in Portland should be notified for possible investigation of a hate crime. The next morning two agents from that office were on the scene.

At the store there were those who were abashed. Doris Bunting was one who said she knew it all along, but no one believed her. Maggie Lassiter asked whether the village should make a formal apology to the Raths, but this was opposed by Bob Pearce and Paul Schissel on the grounds that the town itself had made no formal accusations against them and for instance it was Walter himself who resigned from the selectmen on his own hook and voluntarily, and so it should be up to individuals and not the town as a whole what they might wish to do as concerned apologies. Cal Bowden suggested maybe the selectmen themselves could see if Walter wanted to return to the Board, but this too was argued against as being likely against legal procedures. Herbert Fallows said this was the damnedest situation he could remember, it was like a game with the momentum switching all the time, but he was reminded by Pat Morris that calling it a game was not exactly appropriate, to which Herbert, still hating to lose an argument, suggested a war analogy instead, like the changing tides of battle, which went over with most of the others no better than when he likened what had happened to a game. Kerry Micheau said she was going to bake the Raths a pie and cut Charley's hair for free. This got a laugh out of Doris Bunting, who knew that Charley would never get her hair cut by Kerry, she went down to Portland or Boston or New York to get her hair cut. Meanwhile at the Raths' house Charley stared at the long letter of contrition that she'd written to send to the whole town. It wasn't to be an email, either, it was going out to everybody with an envelope and a stamp. Now she thought to tear it up. It would be a gesture, anyway, tearing it up into small pieces. But better to save it, she thought again, it might one day be a precious fossil, that she could dig out of the ground and decipher something from. She told herself she wasn't angry with the town but more like disappointed, then told herself that people were always telling themselves exactly that when the truth was entirely otherwise. Of course she was angry! And who did it, who set their woods on fire? Walter met with the FBI guys. They asked him if he had anybody in mind who might have had a grudge or had expressed himself in some way, against the project, against the Black kids, against themselves. He recounted the general and fairly reasonable, in his view, all things considered, reluctances of the town. He thought of Donnie Cormer asking if Jews were white people, but chose not to mention it because Donnie was just Donnie, Walter felt he knew him through and through, he was blunt and harmless as a log, and Walter felt if he let his mind go in that direction, every bet he'd made about the world was off. Walter, in a sense, still had faith.

The people of Sneeds took note of the two men from away walking around with "FBI" on the back of their windbreakers and in general felt a certain thrill, as if they were being filmed. But no one had information to offer them. The exceptions to that statement were Donnie and Kevin Cormer, Donnie for what he'd seen and heard from Rine Worsley, and Kevin for what Donnie had told him. Kevin didn't come every day to Sneeds, but when he saw the FBI jackets, he thought it best to talk to his father again. He found him out at the house, five houses down from the burned ones. Donnie was reluctant to talk about any of it, except to say he "gave at the office." Kevin didn't understand what he meant by that but couldn't get Donnie to explain. Donnie was adamant that it was a closed subject as far as he was concerned and people shouldn't be bothering him when they didn't know the whole story of what he'd already done or not done and that was all he was going to say, until Kevin reminded him that the FBI was coming around and it was a crime to lie to them and if they asked Kevin himself if he knew anything, then if only to protect Loozie and the family, he'd have to tell them about the suspicions he'd heard, which frankly he wouldn't want to have to do but when you thought about it, it would also be about honoring Stephen, because whoever set the fire and burned people's houses down as a result, it was like setting fire to Stevie's memory as well. At that point Donnie realized that while he'd given at the office, he hadn't given quite enough. He went back to the pay phone in Ellsworth and added Rine's name to the information he'd previously supplied the sheriff, with the caveat that he couldn't overemphasize that this was no proof whatsoever nor was he accusing anybody of anything. Meanwhile at the Raths' house, Walter and Charley ate a quiet dinner and watched TV. There were times when it seemed they both had the same idea at the same time and this was one of them, as if a clock had struck twelve in their minds when it was only ten past ten. It wasn't even to be noted or remembered who said what first. They would get on the Concordia and sail down the coast, to the tides of Fundy or beyond, maybe go as far north as they could go, out of the country altogether.

Rine Worsley was arrested at a gas station in New Hampshire by state police there. He had finally been farther than Bangor. Because his fingerprints and DNA were subsequently found on a five-gallon gasoline can recovered from a dumpster in Manset, and because tire tracks on the Raths' carriage road matched the tread on the tires of the truck he was driving when arrested, and because he had left a considerable and damning online record of comments about races other than his own, it would never become necessary to determine who dropped the dime on him from a pay phone in Ellsworth. With the threat of a federal indictment overhanging in addition to state charges, he indicated through his court-appointed attorney a willingness to confess and all that remained was to work out the plea bargain. It was all in the paper with his picture.

The Ghosts

In 1893, Hiram Whitlock of Bangor purchased sixty wooded acres in Sneeds Harbor with the intention of building a hotel there to cater to the carriage trade that had recently begun to make Mount Desert Island and other locations on the coast of Maine desirable summer resorts. There was steamer service to Bar Harbor and Whitlock intended to provide private coach transfer from the landing directly to Sneeds, which offered a breezy, healthful climate and invigorating outdoor sporting activities without the hectic clamor of the Bar Harbor social scene. He set about clearing his woods and hired Amelia Janss, one of the first women licensed to practice architecture in the northeastern states, to design a fifty-five-room structure with oriental motifs to suggest the magic of the holy land from which he had recently returned. She produced a plan with turrets and inlaid tiles and quite magnificent arches and other surprises which might call to mind for more imaginative souls the Arabian Nights. It went up in 1895, small gardens lined with orange trees inspired by photographs of the Alhambra were planted, two clay tennis courts were installed beside them, spacious lawns for sitting and tea and croquet were established, and advertisements appeared in *Century* magazine and the like for a new exclusive retreat free from the oppressiveness of the cities equipped with all modern conveniences, private baths en suite, and fireproof to the highest standard.

Whitlock then approached the question of who would staff his new enterprise. A chef was brought from Boston, a hotel manager from Zurich, Switzerland, various tradesmen and apprentices from Bangor, and gardeners and woodsmen from the local area, until the only positions remaining to be filled were in the service area. Here Whitlock was a man of decisive opinions. He had noted many times in his travels abroad that the most elegant establishments might have Africans as room servants, bellhops, and the like, and that especially when in uniform they made a handsome and impressive contrast to their surroundings. His research also led him to believe that they could be clothed and housed and paid at moderate expense. So he advertised in a newspaper written and read by Negroes in New York City for help, offered to pay travel expenses, room and board, and a modest stipend, and touted the advantages to health and well-being of a respite from the city. He soon found himself with eight maids and two all-around handymen.

Nothing is known about the lives of these ten people or those who succeeded them except what can be gleaned from the photographs that were taken of them, the only known copies of which reside in the collections of the Sneeds Harbor Historical Society. They are lined up in two rows in their uniforms. There is a deadness to their eyes, though this is most likely the result of the film's overexposure. They stare as if into nothingness. Their postures are stiff from waiting. The women are young, the men older. If one can gather anything as to whether they were happy or at least satisfied in their positions, it can perhaps be inferred from the fact that many of them returned in the following years. We know the money was minuscule. There are photographs for each year the resort opened. All the photographs are much the same, as if the photographer remained the same or perhaps Hiram Whitlock had a hand in directing their composition. Each year there are exactly eight women and two men. The women were housed in a bunkhouse in back of the kitchens. It's not known where the men stayed. Sneeds had a weekly newspaper during those years and in one edition there's mention of the Negroes working at Sneeds coming into the village for a church fair, from which it may be inferred that such visits were rare occasions. Did they go to church? Did they shop for necessities? Did they mail letters home? Perhaps they did all those things and today they only seem like ghosts, unrecorded except by mystics and in shadows.

The orange trees died the first winter. The Nazareth lasted until March 1902, when it burned overnight. So much for fireproofing to the highest standard, but it being winter, no one was hurt. The hotel was said to have been losing money, a combination of Whitlock's extravagance in his original conception and the stronger pull of the burgeoning Bar Harbor. Arson was suspected but never proved. The woods came back and took over all of it.

The Departure

It was September again when the Raths sailed their white yawl away from Sneeds Harbor. They sailed it up the channel and by the head and past Caitlin's Point and Danny Eastman sat on the rocks on Half Bush and fished for the last of the stripers and saw them sailing towards the sea. It was a morning of tender calm yet all their sails were aloft. Walter hated to motor. And there had never been a time in their lives when there was less place they had to be. Charley watched every bit of land they were leaving. It was as if she wanted to record it, but they were not people to take out their phones, nor had they been for all their years in Sneeds. Walter kept his eyes on the horizon, as if he more than she hated to leave. They crawled along the breeze. Having scattered Stephen's ashes in the bay, it occurred to them both that they were sailing through them. Porpoises came by to say hello or good-bye. The low greens and grays of the land gradually went away.

Paul Schissel, the realtor, got the work of selling the house in the village. It was past the selling season but their asking price was low and Paul knew how to work the Raths' story and what to put in and what to leave out and by Thanksgiving it went to a couple retiring from Pelham Manor, New York. The couple had vacationed on Mount Desert and found Sneeds by accident and fell in love. The Raths kept the camp. There were those who wondered what they intended with it and others who wondered if they would ever come back. It was assumed they kept it because of the stone by the bay and because it was anyway to them small change. There was a sadness in the village about their leaving that no amount of hurt feelings or feelings of rejection or cynicism about people from away and their flightiness or shallowness or money or unsuitability for a certain hardness of life could entirely erase. They left a hole. People in Sneeds did not tend towards the eloquent or sentimental, so it was left to Maggie Lassiter to sum up what many felt. "They did nothing wrong."

And in a few, there was a particular belated regret that went to Charley, for it was she, they knew, who had steered the program through, and been with it all the time, and never quite gave up, and endured the various slings and arrows that had quietly gone her way more than his, as in an old, old story retold. Maggie was in that camp, and Pat, and Kerry, and Francis, all women.

They sailed past Halifax and Cape Breton and through the Cabot Strait and by then they had many times divorced. It would be after dinner or wine when one or the other would find nothing more to say and either he would say she had never wanted the village or she would say he had never wanted the camp or it could have been either of them who remembered that a marriage doesn't survive the death of a child. And why were they together and there was no reason still for them to be together and didn't he wish to go one place and didn't she wish to go another or he to do one thing and she to do another and his thoughts were a bore or his witticisms no longer amused and her outbursts were banal or she didn't get his jokes and if it hadn't been for the child would they have been together to start with and where and how had love fled and paced upon the mountains overhead as the poets said as the playwrights said and on and on and don't stop now while we're still having fun. They made each other a little bit miserable, add that one to the list, a kind of summary, the one-liner for those too lazy to read which those days included themselves. They may have been halfway up the Gulf of St. Lawrence, anchored near nowhere, when Walter came up from the cabin and found her on the bow outside the rail looking down at the dark. It seemed to him she may have been waiting for him to come out to jump.

It was not that it was impossible yet he stayed calm, as if it had all been foreordained. She felt the blackness of the water and considered her chances. Be done with the goddamn thing, fly to heaven through the hole in hell. She who was less than nothing spoke only to herself, in their own secret language that had never been known. The water was everything she dreamed it to be, beckoning, enticing, for real. And Walter took a couple of steps towards her.

"Charley …"

"Right over here," she said.

"Can I come a little closer?"

"Look but don't touch," she said.

"Dinner's ready," he said and took two steps towards her. "Don't you hear the cowbells ringing?"

"You're crazier than I am," she said. "It's no good, Walter."

"It's no good at all," he said.

"Then why bother?" she said.

"You tell me," he said, and took another couple of steps. The deck was damp with the sea dew, so that his shoes slid a little and he feared for her falling by mistake.

"You'll be happier without me," she said. "I absolve you of all responsibility. It's not your fault and it never was."

"That's what they all say," he said.

"Did you really make dinner?" she asked.

"Of course not," he said.

"It's a reasonable thing," she said.

"Dinner or death?" he asked.

"Both of them," she said.

"I suppose they are," he said.

"And you're a reasonable man," she said.

"Not as much as you always thought," he said.

"So I've misunderstood you again," she said.

"I can be as bitter as you if I want to be," he said.

"Don't flatter yourself," she said.

"Please …"

"Pretty please?"

"Not so much."

Her eyes were tiring of the water. It was making her dizzy. There was nothing more to see. There he was. He had taken another couple of steps. Had he always been so old? She saw that he was hoping to outwait her. Her glance shot across the sky like a hose let loose.

"I'm sorry, Walter," she said.

"You spelled my name right," he said.

"Then there's that," she said.

"There was always something," he said.

"One thing or another," she said.

"One thing or another," he repeated.

"It's getting cold," she said.

"Can I get you a jacket?" he asked.

"I'm alright," she said.

"It'll be dark soon," he said.

"It will be," she said.

"If I get you a jacket, will you not go away, will you be here when I get back?"

"I'll wait," she said.

"Then I'll get it," he said.

He turned away so that he couldn't see her and so that she would know he couldn't see her and went below and found a jacket and came back out. She had come back over the rail and was now standing where he had been standing when he left to go below. He put the jacket across her shoulders. They went below. Later they made love in his narrow bunk. It had been a year and they clawed at each other a little and it didn't matter that it wasn't very good. The next day they came about and sailed south, out of the Gulf and into the ocean.

Somewhere on the ocean one night he said to her, "Did you ever want vengeance?" She thought he was talking about the fire but he wasn't. "For Stephen's murder." Pain drew his eyes down and for long enough he couldn't look at her and he pronounced *murder* as if it were almost a word he'd never heard, a word in a foreign language.

"No," she said.

"Lucky you," he said.

"There's no one," she said.

"I know that," he said.

He shivered and couldn't stop shivering. She held his arms but he still didn't stop, so that it seemed he could fall into a thousand pieces.

"It must have been in me all along," he said.

"And you only noticed now?" she said.

"Now. Just now," he said.

She bent closer to him, to see him better, and saw the shame in his eyes.

"The Land of Cockaigne. That was our revenge," she said, and he nodded, and continued to shiver.

And they kept sailing south.

The people from Pelham Manor who came after the Raths were the Baldaccis and within a year they were fitted into the village where her *carbonara* for various occasions was much beloved and he took his regular coffee at the general store, an amiable, talkative sort with a big-city accent. Dick Baldacci came in the store

189

one day to say that he'd seen Walter Rath in New York. Dick had residual business in the city and he remembered Walter from the closing on the house and there he was with his newspaper on the Lexington express from the Bronx. Dick put in here to bolster the credibility of it that people think you'll never run into anyone you know in New York because it's such a vast city but in fact because of the way that the heart of it is so geographically compact, if you have business there you'll often run into someone. And so he had. He was hesitant to approach him because Loretta Baldacci was always telling him he made a fool of himself by so often mistaking ordinary people for celebrities and politicians and the like, but he followed Rath off the train at 59th Street and observed he was wearing falling-apart boat shoes and at that point figured what the hell and give it a shot and accosted him up the stairs to Bloomingdale's. It was indeed Walter, who remembered him and looked well and asked him to say hello to people in Sneeds. They got to the street and Dick was headed into Bloomingdale's and Walter was not, he had an appointment uptown and so hadn't time for a coffee when Dick proposed it. So that was about all Dick knew. They parted cordially. Dick reported that Walter still looked like a country guy, wearing a Patagonia something and smudged khaki pants as well as the boat shoes as if you could take the boy out of the city or vice versa. Doris Bunting wanted to know if he'd grown a beard or anything and Dick said no. Pat Morris asked about Charley and Dick said the hello that Walter sent was from them both, from him and Charley both, but otherwise he had no further information, as they'd only spoken for a minute or two. In point of fact Walter and Charley were living in a two-bedroom apartment on the Grand Concourse, having put their fortune of approximately $311,000,000 into a trust that was slowly giving it away. The boat was gone, most of the rest of their stuff was gone, and what remained was the unfashionable apartment and a commercial building in New Rochelle where Charley went every weekday to sculpt and the camp in Sneeds and just enough money to keep these things going. Most of the trust's gifts so far had been directed to the Bronx Cares Diversionary Action Program, where Walter had become a youth counselor, working the courtrooms and the holding cells of the courthouse each day. The gifts were anonymous, so that Walter suffered no notoriety or deference at work, nor would Sharon Mason ever tell. Charley's work in New Rochelle consisted of vast constructions, attempts to imagine black holes not in their uniformity of loss but as infinite possibility, places of eternal return where you never knew what you might meet up with next and where one of all possible nexts was no next at all. Good luck with that one, she thought, but she went there every day. There had been pictures in the paper of black holes and that had got her going and it all felt like a long time coming. Walter combatted any sense of doing good by continuing to be a curmudgeon in his thoughts. By most counts he was more a curmudgeon than ever, though there was no one really to do the counting but himself. He read Malthus and embraced the thought that the more things went right with mankind, the more they were then bound to go wrong, as men would multiply and eat their way through the earth. He sometimes felt it made him happy to be so disappointed, another count on a bill of indictment as long as the list of Charley's black holes. But what of Malthus? The trap for man was sprung. They watched old movies in the evening like old times and at four in the morning he awoke and worried for the fate of whatever showed up to his mind. War, famine, his Ps going nowhere, skepticism about equality again, skepticism about fraternity again, America's false and sentimental understanding of itself, its pimping, its delusions, its self-intoxication, its ideas that could not stand. And don't get him started again on tech, on the Machine, on the robots colonizing his mind and eating up his brain. Or the world heating up, for that matter, coming to a boil. Would there be a day when we would long for the warmth? Still he would be a Catholic if he could. Still he would be a believer if he could. The moral choice, the freedom of that choice, one thing worth preserving anyway. And was that, too, not going to hell? Charley beside him: wake her and tell her? But tell her what, exactly? Her gentle snore, her face on the pillow, her gaining the strength to live. How unfair to Charley, who would listen, who would nod, who would yearn to get back to her dreams. And why not? It would be four in the morning or five or six. He would read the news on his laptop a little bit and then doze off, the news being somehow soporific, as terrible as it was still somehow a distraction. At seven he would open his eyes and breathe the morning and kiss her forehead or her cheek or her lips if they happened to be available and with a slight dizziness in his first steps go to shower and face the day. Love is an action, not a feeling. Once you go down this path of faith, there is much to be done.

Tim Frobisher had been out lobstering in the bay and it was from there that the word started. He phoned up the store and told Maggie Lassiter. The Raths appeared to be out by the stone they put up there, having a picnic on a blanket. An additional two years had passed from Dick Baldacci's sighting of Walter in New York.

Walter had arrived first. He had rented a car in Bangor and stopped at a market to pick up food, a pilgrim on his way. Three months previous she had gone off and she had chosen not even to tell him where. All they had agreed was that at such-and-such a date and time they would meet at the stone. He had taken the Chinatown bus to Boston and another bus to Bangor, but the rental cars were all at the airport and while he was there he had troubled himself to check the boards for when planes were coming that might be carrying Charley. There was a midday lull with only a flight from Orlando and when she wasn't at the stone at noon he wondered if she would be there at all. Her phone was off. He looked around and tidied up and spread the blanket that he brought. The stone they had chosen was worn and smooth as if it had been around since the continent's beginning and it wasn't granite but Walter had forgotten exactly what it was if it wasn't that. There was no mark on it. They had left it that way so that only the two of them would know its secret song. That was anyway what Charley had said and if he doubted her he didn't say. Now he waited past one o'clock and phoned her again and texted, though he hated to text, and there was nothing, but at just past two another rental car came to the end of the track and parked where his was parked. She was wearing something he loved for her to wear, a sweater in peach with little woolen scarabs woven in it that came not even to her waist and made her look supple and long and as if thirty years hadn't passed. She was late but she didn't say why. She, too, had stopped at a market and brought peaches and other things. They sat on the blanket and ate their lunch and were quiet.

It was then that Tim Frobisher saw them and in truth they saw him as well, or at least his lobster boat puttering from trap to trap as if they'd been hardly gone an afternoon. After lunch they continued the tidying that Walter had begun. A few weeds, a few sticks, a little driftwood. Walter rubbed some seagull shit off the stone. Eventually they told each other a few memories of Stephen, little inconsequential things. They packed up their belongings and their trash at four. Charley kissed the stone and Walter touched it and put a pebble on. He took her hand and they walked to their cars.

Out where the track met the Clarkswood Road, they looked

like a mini caravan coming out of the bush to those who had gathered there. The onlookers were thirty or forty, familiar faces all, spread out along the road. They hadn't wanted to trespass, and as the cars came out they stared and were silent as if they were in a country where tourists were few. Walter, whose car was first, stopped at the head of the track and got out and Charley got out in back of him. They walked towards the crowd. Rose Britton was there, and Maggie Lassiter who had closed the store for the occasion, and Herbert Fallows and Cal Bowden and Pat Morris and even a few whose names Walter had forgotten or never knew. There were a few hugs and embraces but also some standing off, as if the decency of the town required it. Walter said thanks and fixed a smile. Charley hugged Rose in particular, grateful she was still alive and worried she would crush her bones in the embrace. Donnie was there as well, and offered to drive them to Bangor, but they had their cars to return. Not much more was said. People got back in their cars and trucks and drove away.

Walter and Charley drove their rental cars back to the airport and took a cab to the bus station and waited for the bus. She was tired and put her head on his shoulder. Since they had both bought lunch, there was plenty left over for the ride home.

THE END